Witching Moon

by Poppy Woods

Poppy Woods 2019 ©

Cover art by Raven Nordman
Formatting by The Nutty Formatter
Edited by Dani Black

All rights reserved. No part of this book may be reproduced, scanned, or distributed in print or electronic form without express, written permission of the author, except for the use of brief quotations in a book review.

This is a work of fiction. Names, characters, places, and incidents are the product of the author's imagination and any resemblance to any organization, event, or person, living or dead, is purely coincidental.
Except for you. You know who you are.

❋ Created with Vellum

"I think they don't know how to love you correctly."
- Luna

Prologue

I draw my knees up to my chest, my hands wrapped around the warm cup of coffee as I gaze up at the moon. It's utterly silent out here. Beezlebub is a finicky familiar and has never enjoyed sitting with me on nights like tonight—at least not when it's cold outside.

I've always loved the cold. Something about the atmosphere this time of year does something to soothe all the bruises on my soul.

And this year, there had been a *lot* of those.

Sure, the normal family drama filled the year to the brim with fresh traumas, but I'm almost used to those hurts at this point in my life. What broke my soul in new and inventive ways this year was Jess.

It's one thing to break up because something is *broken* in your relationship. It's a completely different scenario when everything is fine and one of you decides to leave and move across the country. Although, the argument could be made if we were so happy, Jess would have never left.

I groan, shaking my head as the moonlight falls across my legs. It's supposed to snow tomorrow, the temperature will drop even lower as the winter storms set in. I love the snow, but clear nights like tonight make my soul sing.

The crisp air biting at my cheeks, a nice warm mug of coffee or hot cocoa, fuzzy pants, and a big moon to listen to all my problems. Yep. My favorite time of year.

"I wish she hadn't left. I wish I was enough," I whisper to the wind.

People say the Moon can hear your troubles, and its spirit will calm you and ease any trouble you might have.

I don't know if I believe that, but I do believe in the peace it brings. There's something to be said for anything that makes your heart feel lighter, I think.

"She couldn't have loved me," I admit out loud with a heavy sigh. Something in my chest feels like it's cracking to pieces all over again as that realization sets in. "At least, not like I loved her. I would have never left her."

But I didn't go with her, either.

That thought rolls back and forth across my mind like a bowling ball, knocking over every positive, logical thought that came before. Heaviness settles in the pit of my stomach like a stone. I'm familiar with that feeling.

Grief.

"I guess you can mourn people even when they're alive," I laugh, wiping at the moisture building in my eyes. I was mourning often these days.

We were about to buy our own house, move in together, and really make a go of things. At first, my family didn't approve of Jess being human, but they eventually came around. After all, I'm more like her than I am like them.

Jess and I are opposites in almost every way. She's a cute, thin, science nerd and I'm a chunky musician. I laugh as images of her getting her hair dyed pink and blue skitter through my mind. She'd done it to try and prove she could be 'edgy'. Silly human.

"She's gone and she's not coming back." I nod solemnly as if agreeing with myself. "It's time I let her go."

"Yeah, it is," Laney's soft voice murmurs from behind me. I crane my neck around to get a look at her. My little sister adjusts the light-weight jacket to cover her shoulders as she looks at me.

"What are you doing out here, Firefly?" My eyebrow raises as I notice she's barefoot, but I know better than to comment. Laney's fire magic keeps her warmer than the rest of us, even when she isn't actively using it.

"I had a feeling you could use some company." She plops down in the empty chair beside me and pulls her knees up to her chest, wrapping her arms around them. "That, and Beezlebub kept muttering at me from the windowsill."

"He won't come out here in the cold unless he absolutely has to."

"Apparently, he thinks I'm a good substitute," Laney grumbles.

I snort and shake my head. "I'm fine. I just like to come out here and think, you know that."

"Yeah, but you've been doing it a lot lately, Bug," Laney whispers. "Are you going to be okay?"

"I think so." I shrug, it's not like I know how long it's going to take me to get over what happened. Losing Jess, in the middle of all of our plans finally coming true, broke something deep inside me.

"You know I'm here right?"

"I know," I yawn against the back of my hand. "I just need time, I think."

"Bug, it's been three months."

I blink as that fact is shoved into my conscious mind for the first time. Had it really been so long since Jess moved to California? That inconvenient truth makes my admissions tonight ring even more true. It's time to let Jess go. It's time to move on with my life.

I've been in a rut since we ended things. I haven't been making music like I should. That's another thing I have to get back on track with. This . . . hole in my heart has eaten up my *passion*. And that's not okay.

"What are you thinking about over there?" Laney asks, propping her chin on her hand.

I sit my coffee cup down and lean forward, leaning my elbows on my knees. "All the things I need to do to let this go."

"For starters, you need to stop talking to her."

"That's easier said than done. We were in love—"

"I know you loved her, Bug. But she left. She knew you couldn't go with her, she knows California isn't a safe state for our kind and she took the job anyway. If that doesn't tell you where you fall on her list of priorities, then I don't know what will."

I blink away moisture as it gathers in the corner of my eyes. She's right. I'd said basically the same thing not five minutes ago, but it still hurts to hear it come from someone else. Especially so bluntly.

"I didn't even try to go with her. I could probably pass as human, if I wanted to," I mumble. Defending Jess has been second nature for so long, I can't help it.

"You're right. You didn't."

I stare at my sister, my mouth falling open as her words slap me across the face. Did she really just blame me for this? Just as anger begins to boil in my chest and I purse my lips to retaliate, Laney holds up a hand, signalling for me to wait.

"If you loved her as much as you think you did, you would have tried. If she loved you as much as she said, she wouldn't have put you in the position to have to. Sometimes, things just aren't meant to be." Her voice is soft and sad and I can't help but let her words sink deep into my spirit.

I nod, turning away from her. I prop my feet up on the porch rail as I gaze up at the clear sky. The first of the snow clouds can be seen in the distance, making their way toward the sleepy little coven-town of Waitsfield, Vermont, but for right now, everything is peaceful.

Everything except my heart.

Help me move past her, I beg the Moon silently. *Help me get back to the person I used to be.*

If there was anything I'd learned over the years about relationships—with significant others or family—it was that toxicity could twist you into someone you're not. It's hard to see it happening in the moment, but one day you look back and don't recognize the person you are compared to who you were when you started out.

This is one of those nights.

Laney doesn't say anything else, just sits with her knees pulled up against her chest like a child while I stare up at the sky. I wonder for a moment if the answers I need are out there somewhere in the universe where I can't reach.

Chapter 1
Alandra

I squeeze into my seat at the table. The one nearest the wall, smushed in so I can't escape, has always been my spot at the Michaels' family dinner table. To my left, my sister sits, smiling at our father, talking about some amazing thing she's done since the last time we saw them.

Laney has always been the golden child, the raven haired prodigy with a fire affinity which rivals the eldest members of our community. I, on the other hand, have always been completely fucking normal. Sure, I can practice magic. I can say the right words, sprinkle the right herbs, do the math required to make some magic happen . . . but I have no natural affinity. My father is one of the strongest Telekinetics to ever be born and my mother is a famed Medium. Everyone expects their children to be great and yet, here we are.

"Alandra?" Mom hisses across the table. "How was your week, sweetheart?" She looks to the side for a second and a chill rushes down my spine. It's unnerving, knowing spirits are always around her. It bothered me as a child and it still bugs me. I mean, honestly, what's to stop some pervy ghost from telling my mother something she has no business hearing? I shudder as thoughts of ghostly peeping toms drift through my head.

My hand slides nervously up my neck and bumps into Beezlebub. He chitters against my ear before flitting off across the dinner table. That moth might be my familiar, but he has absolutely no manners. "It was okay. I managed to land a new client."

"Oh? That's exciting!" Dad murmurs, setting his fork down. "Anyone we'd know?"

"Uh," I mutter, looking to Laney for help. She has her nose buried in her cell phone—texting Marcus no doubt—and doesn't make any move to save me from the inquisition. "I doubt it, honestly. He's a pretty new rapper, but everyone seems to expect big things from him. He uses classical music as backdrops to his freestyles."

Dad blinks at me across the table. If it wasn't for the growl that echoes beneath us, I'd never know he was upset. He's always been amazing at compartmentalizing his emotions and saving the reactions for a later, more strategic date. Diego, however, doesn't care about social niceties. The wolf beneath the table lets out a quiet whuff, ending on another growl and my father clicks his tongue, commanding the animal to stop.

Familiars are tied to their witches and their magic. The more powerful the familiar, the more powerful the witch, or so they say. Or maybe the more powerful the witch, the more powerful the familiar. I watch Beezlebub dart around the kitchen. He's extremely large for a moth, and clearly magical with his exaggerated and oversized features, but he's still an insect. Mom's raven isn't in the house, she likes to sit outside, but I know she's lurking around here somewhere.

"That sounds—" Mom pauses, glancing to Dad before she clears her throat. "Promising. Have you considered our offer to put you into the herbalist program in Mont Pelier?"

My teeth grind together as I shake my head. I have absolutely no intention of going to school to be an herbalist. There are plenty of herbalists in our community. *I should be used to this by now, what's wrong with me?* As my phone vibrates in my pocket, I quickly realize the answer. I've been on edge since Jess left. It's not like that should be some huge realization, honestly. A breakup like that one will probably stay with me for a while.

"I think it'd be wonderful if you took on a more traditional role, like your sister," Dad interjects, drawing my eyes back to him.

"I'm not very traditional," I remind him, straightening my spine. I try to ignore the cold blue eyes that meet mine, but it's impossible. Sterlen Michaels commands attention, no matter what he does. It's one of the things that has made him so successful. Magical law can be tricky to practice, but my father has found a foothold in our community that's unprecedented.

"And maybe that's part of the problem—"

"Sterlen!" Mom snaps, turning to look at him. I roll my eyes and start to shimmy out of my chair. There's not much room between the table and the wall and my hip bumps into the former, sending a cup of tea rocketing onto its side. Everyone jumps up quickly, the table sliding into my hip again from all the commotion.

"Fuck!" I snarl, shoving it away as I slide out from between the wall and the deathtrap as quickly as possible. My hands slip into my back pockets—a nervous habit—and I shrug apologetically. I'd do something to help, but Dad already has a towel swirling around the table, sopping up the mess I made. He clasps his hands in front of his mouth, as if in deep thought while the towel moves across the surface of its own volition.

"I just worry, is all. We want what's best for you, Bug," he finally whispers, meeting my eyes again. His are much softer now.

"I know, Dad," I sigh, looking away. I hate the pitiful look he gets when we talk about my magic, or lack thereof.

"Things are different for you. I just want you to have a fulfilling life." I know he means it. The pained look on his face, the proof of his sincerity, doesn't make me feel any better about his pity.

The truth is I'm perfectly happy with the amount of magic I have. Could I be more fabulous with an affinity? Sure. But this is who I am. There's nothing I can do to change it, which I know because my family has tried for years, and I don't know any different. It's hard for them to imagine being average, but for me? It's everyday life.

"I know, Dad."

"I just—"

"Sterlen, stop," Mom pleads. She's always felt the same way he does, but she's better at hiding her disappointment over my normalcy. Michaels are expected to do great things. Laney teaches children how to control their affinity and tutors fire affinities privately. She's highly respected in Waitsfield and across the witching community.

I'm just a musician. And not even a *serious* one. Sometimes I wonder if I joined an opera if my family would be happier with my career. A part of me knows they'll always want me to do better, though. I push my hair behind my ear, trying to ignore the quiet bickering between my parents.

Laney pokes my side and I lean against the back of her chair. "I'm going to head out, I'll see you at the house."

"Bye, Bug," she whispers with a sad smile. At least we'd taken separate cars.

Wiggling my fingers in goodbye, I turn toward the door as I unclip my keys from my belt loop. The soft feeling of Beezlebub landing on the back of my shoulder comforts me. He sends all of the positive energy he can muster and it flows through my back and into my being. He can't speak to me, but I can feel his sympathy in the warm gesture.

"At least she isn't a null," Mom whisper screams to my father.

My hand stills on the door handle and my shoulders sag under the weight of my family's expectations. If they could just accept me for who I am, things would be so much easier. I shake my head and pull the door open, ignoring the sounds behind me.

No doubt, my mom would call and apologize later. *Null.* How could she? Snow crunches beneath my boots as I trudge toward my car. I steel my spine and hop in, cranking the engine fast. I don't want to deal with their apologies tonight. I'm maxed out emotionally, something I'm finding happens a lot more frequently than it used to. Between everything that happened with Jess and her big move across the country and my usual family drama, I'm just tired. Bone deep tired. The kind of tired sleep can't fix.

THE LIGHT FROM MY HEADLIGHTS REFLECTS OFF THE SMALL HOUSE AS I pull into the drive. It's a modest sized home for upper Vermont. Most of the houses in Waitsfield are bigger than ours, but Laney and I like it. It was one of the few houses in our price range when we moved out of our parents' home that was still close by.

For some reason, living completely across town seemed daunting at the time. Now, I wish we'd moved to Timbuktu.

"I can't believe she compared me to a null," I hiss into the wind as I step out of the car and slam the door behind me. Beezlebub bumps into the side of my cheek before taking off toward the house. He hates the snow. I love it.

I unlock the door, drop my keys into the bowl on the tiny table Laney insisted we buy, and stomp through the house to the back door. Pulling it open, I glance over my shoulder for Beezlebub, but he's nowhere to be found. "Thanks, bud," I whisper sarcastically as I step out onto the covered patio.

You really can't beat the views in Vermont.

I take a deep breath, watching the snowflakes fall around me as I stare at the heavy moon in the distance. Yule will be starting soon. The sun sets earlier and earlier each day. Nighttime has always pulled at something deep inside my bones, like what little magic resides inside me recognizes something equally ancient in the darkness.

My phone vibrates in my pocket again and this time I pull it out, staring at the name on the screen: JessyBae. My nose wrinkles as I swipe away the notification. I don't want to talk to her. She left, and I don't necessarily blame her because it's amazing that she's chasing her dream, but things are different now. We aren't together, and calling and texting me constantly to remind me our situation sucks isn't going to make it easier for me to move on.

Laney is right. I need to let her go, to rip the Band-Aid off and just end all communication. It's going to be hard, especially at first, but I think it's what's necessary for me to heal. Even as the thought concretes itself into my mind, guilt stifles my chest.

"What the hell else am I supposed to do? I can't go be with her," I whisper to the quiet night. But no one answers me. There's no one to listen. Just the moon.

Chapter 2
Alandra

I adjust the headphones so they fit snugly around my ears and press play. This track took me forever to compose because my client has a specific sound in mind. It should be frustrating, going back and forth, but honestly, I love the dude's vision.

He wants what he wants. I can respect that. As I drag the recording of his vocals and drop it onto the classical background, I close my eyes and let myself get lost in the music for a moment. He's new. He's talented, but not talented enough that he's going to blow up on his own. No, he'll need to promote the hell out of himself to get anywhere in the industry. These lyrics, though.

My head bobs with the rhythm of his words even as they work against the music I created. It's volatile. It's uncomfortable.

It's perfect.

I glance at the screen and attach the file in an email, say a silent prayer to the Goddess he loves it as much as I do and wait. The wait is the worst part of anything, as my Grandma used to say. I miss her, sometimes. She never questioned me, my decisions, or my magic.

"There's a strength in you that wouldn't exist if you were like your sister." Her voice rings in my head, as clear as day. I like to think moments like this are more than memories, that it's her way of reaching out to me from the other side, but I know I'm not a medium.

"It would be easier if I were," I sigh as I click through my screens, looking for something on social media. A small red notification appears in the bottom right corner of my screen and I flinch. It's like being prodded over and over again by something sharp enough to hurt, but not sharp enough to break the skin.

Jess sent me an email. I hover over the notification with the mouse and read the message preview:

Landra, I miss you. I know what we said, but I just really need to talk to someone who gets it. Will you please call me back? Text me? Email? Smoke signals? Something. I feel like you hate me now. We were best friends before we were together . . .

MY FINGER HESITATES ON THE MOUSEPAD. I'M MORE THAN A LITTLE tempted to read the rest of her message, even though I know I shouldn't do it. A clean break is the only way to deal with something like this. Jess and I hadn't broken up because of anything wrong in our relationship. *That's what makes this so fucking hard*, I think to myself for the thousandth time. We were planning on moving in together in a few months, but then she got the job offer which changed everything.

A research position in California. It was great for her, but it also meant the end of our relationship. The only witching communities in California are Hellenistic and they aren't a fan of other sects.

Being a human, Jess couldn't wrap her head around why I didn't want to move out there. She didn't understand that being a solo practitioner was hard, especially for someone like me with no natural affinity. Sure, most humans are fairly tolerant—or they possess a healthy amount of fear that prevents them from screwing with our kind—but when you're on your own with no reflexive magic, things can get scary. Fast.

My head tilts to the side. I know I didn't hear anything in the house—the rooms are all soundproofed with spellwork—but something tells me there's someone here.

As I creep toward the door, more cautiously than I normally would, I grab my cell phone from the dresser. "Laney?" I call out once the door squeaks open. There's no answer. I glance down at my phone and cringe. I didn't realize how late it had gotten. With a sigh, I pad down the hallway toward the living room and kitchen.

I freeze at the corner, taking in the sight before me. Laney is sprawled across the couch, her legs draped haphazardly over the end with one shoe barely dangling from her toes. My eyebrows draw down into a scowl as I march toward her, ready to lay into her for drinking so much on a Monday.

"Shhh, she's sleeping," someone hisses in warning from the kitchen.

I jump, spin around, and raise my hands up as if I know some kind of karate. I don't, but whoever the hell is in my house doesn't know that. "Who the fuck—"

"It's just me, calm down," the voice laughs, stirring some herbs into a glass of tea. My eyes take a second to register the person standing in front of me is in fact Marcus, Laney's boyfriend.

I lay a hand over my chest and shake my head, just staring for a second. "You're too damn big to be sneaking up on people like that," I mutter.

Marcus' eyes crinkle as he smiles, stirring the tea with a swirl of his finger above the cup. He's a Telekinetic like my father. It's annoying on an entirely different level. I narrow my eyes on him, dismissing the threat I'd originally registered when I entered the room. He really is tall, I note, as if to make myself feel better for panicking. Laney had said he was like six foot four or something ridiculous like that. I squeeze into the small kitchen beside him and open the refrigerator, searching for something to drink. I hadn't realized I was thirsty until I saw him making tea.

"She went a little too hard tonight." Marcus props himself against the counter. His eyes bore into the side of my head until I turn to face him. My fingers twist the cap off a fizzy water and I shrug, meeting his pale blue gaze. Marcus has a tendency of looking intense and it makes me uncomfortable because I feel like he's seeing more than he should. His dark hair, slightly crooked nose, and pale skin don't remind me of a vampire villain, but the way his skin clings so tightly to his cheekbones does. It gives his face this illusion of being all angles and makes him look more like a weapon than a man.

"Big surprise."

"You don't have to judge her so much, you know," he sighs. "It's hard for her."

"Sure it is," I snort before taking a swig of the carbonated water.

"Hopefully this helps her sober up some. She actually worried me tonight." Marcus nods toward the cup of tea with an apprehensive smile.

I sit the bottle down and wrap my hands around the teacup he's holding with a sigh. Before I can pull the cup completely from his grasp, his free hand comes down on mine, brushing his fingers over the back of my hand. My skin crawls under his touch.

"You just need to be easier," he murmurs and I have a feeling he's referring to more than just Laney.

"You're not exactly my type," I laugh, hoping he's joking. I've never liked him but I've never been able to put my finger on why, until now. It's beyond inappropriate for him to be treating me so intimately. For one, he knows I'm gay. For two, his girlfriend is passed out drunk not fifteen feet away from us. And for three, said girlfriend happens to be my sister!

"You wouldn't be the first woman to change her mind for the right one." I search his face for any sign showing he's joking, but he isn't and it takes every ounce of self-control I possess not to knock the arrogant douche in the mouth. "You just have to say yes once," he whispers, his voice dripping with a promise that makes my stomach turn.

I manage not to hit him but I can't stop the shudder that makes my head twitch as I yank the cup from his hand and retreat to the living room. My nose drifts side to side over the cup, trying to identify the smell. I realize I don't know what all he put in the tea as I crouch down beside the couch.

"Laney, wake up," I hiss, shoving her shoulder gently. "I need you to drink this." *And to get your dude under control.*

"It'll detox her," Marcus calls from the kitchen over the sound of cabinet doors opening and closing.

What the hell is he doing in there now?

"Mm?" Laney mumbles, swatting at my hand as she rolls over onto her side. Grinding my teeth, I slide my hand under her neck to the back of her skull and lift her up, little by little while she protests. "Let me sleep!"

"You've got to stop doing this." I shake my head, pushing the cup toward her mouth. She reeks of liquor. "I can't believe you let her get this drunk," I snap, hoping Marcus can hear me.

"She's grown."

"She has a problem."

"No, I fucking don't!" Laney snarls, snatching the cup from my hand so fast some hot tea splashes onto my arm. I jerk backward, staring at her in disbelief. She's so fucked up she can barely hold the damn cup in her hands but of course, she doesn't have a problem.

"Whatever!" I throw my hands up in the air, admitting defeat and stomp my way down the hall. When I get to my room, I slam the door closed for extra effect. I'm tempted to scream at the door, but it's not like they'd hear me if I did.

No one has ever listened to me about Laney's drinking problem. At first, I thought I was being a good sister by helping her sneak back into the house when she was too drunk to do it herself. But as the years went on, and late high school parties turned into week-long-college-binges, I realized I was actually enabling her.

I pull the phone from my back pocket and flick to my mom's contact. It's so tempting to call her, but Marcus is right. Laney is an adult and nothing is going to change until she is ready for it to change. I click the screen off and lay the phone down on the dresser.

It's dark in the room except for the glow of the computer screen and the moonlight splashing across my bed. Shaking my head as another skeevy shudder racks my spine, I try to push the weird encounter with Marcus out of my head.

"I'm going to have to tell her about that tomorrow," I groan to no one. Beezlebub chitters softly across the room and I find myself looking for him. When a shadow darkens the computer screen, I move to my desk, slumping down in the chair. "What do you think, man?"

The oversized moth just stares at me, perched precariously on the corner of my screen. A new red notification catches my eye and I slide the mouse over to see who it's from.

Ally! That's dope as fuck! Thanks man!

I roll my eyes at the nickname but a smile still creeps across my face. At least someone is happy with me right now. Even if it's just a client.

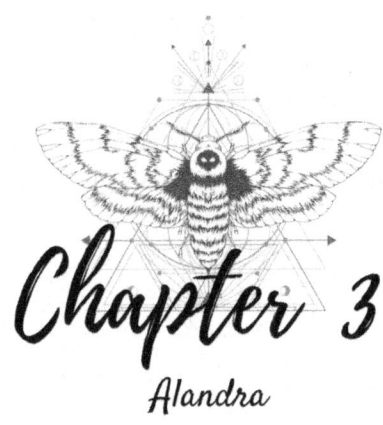

Chapter 3
Alandra

I wake up to the sound of yowling. With a groan, I roll over and come face to face with Beezlebub. Fuzzy grey hair covers most of his body, interspersed only by the darker grey of some of his markings and deep blood red designs that he's known for. The fur around his mouth twitches as he stares at me with unblinking eyes and I roll mine.

"Good morning, B." He rubs his two front feet together in a gesture I've come to think of as 'hello' over the years.

Another loud yowl tears through the house and I rub my temples. The rooms are soundproofed—magically soundproofed no less—how the hell can I hear Juniper? I swing my feet over the side of the bed and Beezlebub flutters his wings but makes no move to get up.

"Lazy."

A surge of amusement courses through me and I know it's not my own. No, it's got to be Beezlebub's because I'm annoyed as fuck.

I stomp down the hallway, my arms crossed over my chest. My sock covered feet slide to a stop on the smooth wooden floor as I enter the living room to see Laney mid-argument with her familiar.

"Juniper!" she snaps, reaching for something the snow leopard has in her mouth. "Give it back!"

Leaning against the wall, I decide to watch instead of intervening. When I heard Juniper screaming, I'd thought something was wrong, but watching a very hungover Laney chase a seventy-five pound cat is free, wholesome entertainment.

"You could help." Laney doesn't even turn toward me when she says it. I roll my eyes and pad toward the large leopard with a smile.

"Whatcha got for Auntie Alandra?" I ask, bracing my hands on my knees. My most annoying baby voice takes over. "Whatcha got? Wanna gimme? Gimme it." I hold out one hand and wait, smiling at the beautiful cat as she bounces back and forth away from my sister before running toward me.

My fingers find the scruff of her neck as I pet her, holding her still while Laney rushes over to fish out whatever's in her mouth. "That's a bad kitty," I coo at the oversized house cat.

"She chewed my fucking charger to pieces," Laney growls, glaring at her familiar. "She's been doing this so much lately!"

"Probably because you're always on your phone." I shrug. The truth was, Juniper had been eating chargers since Laney started seeing Marcus. The fact that she has to lock Juniper in her bedroom or out of the bedroom when Marcus is over should be a big, fat, flashing warning sign. Leave it to my sister to ignore it for a pretty face.

"I don't understand why she's so mad. I've dated before. I wonder if it's because she can sense how serious Marcus and I have gotten. Maybe she's jealous."

I snort, drawing a death glare from Laney and try to cover it with a cough. Her usually perfect, raven colored hair is jutting out in every direction this morning. It's obvious she hasn't touched it since she woke up. Having a pixie-cut will do that to you. Those cuts take the kind of dedication I can't commit to. My fingers comb through my own platinum colored waves.

My hair looks bleached at first glance, especially standing next to my sister, but it's all natural. Our father has straw blonde hair and our mother has dark hair like Laney's. For some reason, my genes had decided to wreak havoc.

"So, why exactly could I hear Juniper in my bedroom?"

"I needed your help, so I took the barrier down for a sec." Laney shrugs, patting Juniper on the side before she stands back up to her own full height, which isn't much. Laney is tiny. She's always been tiny and she always will be. I've seen the girl wolf down enough food to give a teenage boy a bellyache and she still hasn't gained a pound since highschool.

Perfect.

"Well, put it back up so I can go back to sleep," I mutter, turning toward the hall again.

"*Silentium*," she whispers. A chill runs down my spine as the power in the house shifts. "You know the words, why didn't you just do it?"

"Not my spell." I shrug.

"You know what today is, right?"

"Yes, Laney. Yule starts tonight." I roll my eyes, pulling the ends of my sleeves down over my fingers. It's chilly in the living room this morning.

"Okay. Just making sure." She takes a deep breath, looks down at the tattered charging cable still clutched in her palm, and then throws it onto the couch with a look of disgust. "I need you to bless the house tonight. Marcus' family is having a small celebration and he wants me to come over." She pushes an unruly strand of hair away from her face and tucks it behind her ear, looking at me with the *'please'* eyes.

My own eyes narrow on her, I'm ready to lay into her about what a creep Marcus is when it hits me. She asked me to bless the house. My jaw goes slack and whatever I was about to say dies on the tip of my tongue.

"You want me to what?"

Laney sighs dramatically and moves toward the kitchen. Juniper stalks off, probably looking for Beezlebub to annoy, and I follow Laney apprehensively.

"The spell is on the fridge." She points to the piece of paper secured by a small pentagram shaped magnet. I squint at the tiny cursive lettering and nod, sliding a hand into my hair at the base of my neck. No one has ever asked me to do anything like this before on my own. I'm not a *null*, but I'm also not talented. This feels . . . *great*. "It's really important to invoke the Moon's protection through the long nights, Bug. Please don't forget." Laney glances from me to the spell on the fridge, worry creasing her brow.

The dark circles under her eyes worry me. I want to lecture her about being irresponsible, but I can't. She trusts me to bless the house.

"What do you think is going to get us if we don't protect the house during Yule?" I snicker lightheartedly. "The boogeyman?"

"Bug," she whines. "Do I need to stay home and do it? I'll just tell Marcus I can't come."

I throw my hands out over hers and shake my head. "No, no! I got it! It's fine." I don't tell her that her boyfriend is a mega creep who thinks he can flirt with anything that moves, including her sister. I don't tell her I'm a nervous wreck over her trusting me with this. I don't want anything to ruin this moment, even if that's selfish.

"Are you sure?" She points to a smaller piece of paper tacked to bottom of the spell. "This is a list of herbs we don't have at the house and need for the spell. You'll probably have to go into town to get them."

"No problem." My mouth stretches wide with a grin. Not only over the fact that Laney is asking me to do this, but also over the fact that she's so damn nervous about it. It's a simple blessing. How fucking hard could it be? But I'm too excited to be offended.

Laney rubs her temples, her perfectly manicured nails digging into the skin as she groans. "Okay, I have to go get ready. You promise you've got this?"

"Yesssss," I drawl out. "Shoo."

Laney walks out of the kitchen and disappears down the hall. Scanning the list of ingredients one more time, I make a mental note to get into town before sunset. The herbalist—Greda—is a traditional old witch and will be at home preparing for Yule as soon as the moon rises.

SEND.

There. At least the invoice for the project was finally done. Once I receive the funds, I can release the full file to the artist. I'm really proud of my work on that track. Even though the idea belongs solely to the artist, being a part of the creation process is amazing. Every time I open an email from a happy client, a warmth spreads through me. An even sweeter feeling rushes through me whenever I get an email from someone saying they were *recommended* by a happy client.

I guess I'm so used to fucking everything up, I cling to any kind of positive feedback I can get my greedy fingers on.

Some of my clients aren't ever going to be big names. That's just the nature of the business. Music is ridiculously hard to break into. But I'm equally proud of the small-town bands who buy my pre-made clips for their songs.

"There's a way to make money off anything on the internet," I laugh as Beezelbub lands on top of my head. "What the hell do you think you're doing?" His wings rub together, a soft but aggravating sound that reverberates through my ear.

"What?" I hiss, swatting at my head.

Fumbling for my phone, terror seizes me before I even pull the screen up to my face. *Oh my Goddess, it's so fucking late!* I check the time, just to reinforce how fucked I am before I cringe, leaping from the chair and out the bedroom door. I snatch my keys from the bowl by the door and rush toward the car, still pulling my jacket around my shoulders. I'm not even sure where Beezlebub is at this point, I'm so frantic.

My feet slide across a particularly icy portion of the driveway and I curse under my breath, throwing my hands out to catch my balance before fall flat on my ass.

"Laney trusted you, you fucking idiot," I groan as I slide the key into the ignition. The sun behind the trees glows the dark orange that it does at sunset. There's no way I'm going to make it to the shop in time, I realize, with a heavy heart. I pull my phone from my pocket and bring up the number for the herbalist.

Maybe if I can catch her before she leaves, she'll wait.

Ring!

Ring!

Ring!

Ring!

A crackling sound like a candy being unwrapped comes across the line before a sweet elderly voice begins speaking. "Thank you for calling Thistles and Thorns. We are either closed or with another customer! Please leave your name, number, and a brief description of what you're looking for and someone will get back to you as soon as possible."

I end the call before the tell-tale beep can sound in my ear. *For fuck sakes!* My fingers drum against the steering wheel as I stare at the house and wonder what to do. There's got to be something I can substitute the missing ingredients with; there usually is.

The key snags in the ignition before it finally releases and I pop the car door open, trekking back across the driveway to the front door. My hand twists the knob and I realize in my hurry to leave I didn't lock the door. *Stupid.*

I kick off my now snow-covered shoes and make my way into the kitchen, opening the cabinet that reveals two different spice racks. One holds herbs and spices used for cooking, one holds herbs used for witching. There's some crossover, especially with things like sage, but for the most part, we keep them separated in the house.

Making a quick inventory of what we have on hand, I turn back toward the refrigerator and pull down the note from Laney.

"Hmm," I hum, tapping my finger on my chin. "We don't have cardamom or cedar." I turn back to the cabinet, searching the available herbs for a worthy substitute.

My eyes fall on the chickweed and calamus. Calamus is commonly used in moon magic and has its uses for protection, too. It should do the trick. A streak of dark grey and red grabs my attention and I turn in time to see Beezlebub land on the cabinet beside the one I'm rummaging through. I swear he looks like he's judging me.

"What is it?" Pulling the two containers down from the shelf, I look back at the spell and begin gathering the rest of the ingredients. I double check everything and scoop it into my arms, making my way to the living room. We'd built a beautiful altar into the house when we bought it. The nook jutting out from the window that faced the front yard was perfect and we'd quickly repurposed it for our own use.

As I try to sit everything down, the single white candle necessary for the spell rolls onto the altar, bumping into the metallic candle holder. I cringe, knowing I'd get yelled at for that if anyone had seen. Everything on the altar is meant to be in balance. Any chaos can ruin the spell, change the outcome of it, and even bring about some dire consequences. Unfortunately, I have first hand experience with this particularly disturbing fact.

The altar is already dressed for Yule. Sprigs of greenery adorn the window sill directly behind the space where we practice our magic. A Yule log, dressed and ready for the holiday, rests against the window, waiting for the solstice. Laney prepared all of this well before we needed it. Yule is her favorite time of year, and we've always celebrated together, ever since we left our parents' house.

That's why it's so odd she's spending time with Marcus and *his* family tonight instead. I sigh, forcing the thoughts from my head. I know I need to set my intention.

I survey the set up with a solemn nod. "Looks good, right B?"

Beezlebub flaps his wings slowly where he clings to the wall and I roll my eyes. I adore him, don't get me wrong. But what kind of witch has a *moth* for a familiar? A house cat is common. A dog would be strange, but not unheard of. Snakes happen sometimes. Birds, especially ravens, are very common, even wolves make more sense than a moth.

Once the candle is properly dressed, I combine the herbs into the tiny cauldron and light it with a charcoal disc. Goosebumps rush down the back of my neck and I shiver, looking around the room as if someone is watching.

"You're a huge help," I mutter to Beezlebub, ignoring the annoyance surging through the back of my mind. He definitely understands sarcasm. I make my way through the house, turning off each light I find still on. The only one remaining is the dim light in the living room.

Sinking to my knees in front of the altar, I light the white candle. The smell of frankincense is strong. My poor nose protests but I power through it as I recite the spell.

> *"As we approach the year's longest night*
> *I ask you, Goddess, for your light,*
> *Cast our home in your moonlit presence,*

Granting us your glowing essence.

For we shall be under your lunar protection,
Keeping out those with ill intention,
Bless us through the darkest hours,
With your otherworldly powers.

We welcome you into our nights,
To bless us, guard us, until the return of light.

As I will it, so mote it be,
Thank you, Goddess, and blessed be."

SPELLWORK IS MY ONLY REAL CONNECTION TO MAGIC AND THE sensation will never get old. An enticing shiver winds around my spine as I repeat the words a second time. The levels of power in the room shifts as the third repetition begins. I've never lead the ceremony, maybe this is how Laney and Mom feel every year.

"Thank you, Goddess, and blessed be," I whisper, picking up the candle snuffer from the alter. As I cover the open flame, smoke billows threateningly out of the cauldron, much more than should be possible for such a small thing. I wave my hands around, coughing as the grey-blue smoke fills the room.

"Fuck!" I cover my mouth and nose, rushing toward the door and pull it open. Cold air blasts in the room but I'm less worried about catching pneumonia than I am about suffocating. I fan the smoke with the door, shoving it almost closed then opening it again quickly, trying to suction it all from the room. It takes a few tries to get enough suction to move the smoke at all, and it doesn't seem to be enough to suck it out of the living room. Eventually Beezlebub gets involved. I can see his wings causing curls in the smoke as he darts around the room and *finally* the smoke begins to thin.

Coughing against my hand, I continue to fan the last bits of smoke from the house. I turn toward the altar, trying to remember where I left off in the spell and my eyes go wide as they land on an unfamiliar figure in the middle of my personal space.

"Who the fuck are you?" I shriek, my hand covering my heart as if it might leap from my chest. And in truth, it might. For a multitude of reasons. My heart hammers against my palm as hard as it can as I survey the stranger in my living room.

She's taller than me and pale. Her long white hair hangs down her back in loose, bouncing waves. I swallow, trying to skip over the shape of her breasts in the sheer white dress she's wearing. The woman is beauty personified. But all of that aside—

Her eyes meet mine and everything ceases for a moment. I instantly regret speaking so harshly to her. The pale blue—no not blue, not quite—eyes looking back at me are full of confusion.

"Wh—who are you, hot stuff?" I try again, pushing my hair behind my ear. I'm equal parts confused, terrified, and interested in the strange woman standing in my living room. "How'd you get in here?" I don't move from the door, my left hand still clasping the cold metal firmly in case I need to make an escape.

"I'm Luna," she murmurs, spinning in a slow circle to look around the room. Her face is pure bewilderment. I'm not sure what she's so impressed with, our house is modest on its best day.

"Luna who?" I press. "How the hell did you get in here?"

"Mortals sure are surlier than I remember," she huffs, coming to a sudden stop with her arms crossed over her chest. Her eyebrow arches as her eyes once again meet mine and a zing of electricity arcs down my back.

"Excuse me?" Beezlebub lands softly on the stranger's shoulder and she turns to face him, running a finger down his fuzzy body.

"Hello!" Her voice sounds lyrical, like she's talking to a baby. Beezlebub chitters contentedly at her and I narrow my eyes. *Traitor.* I have to admit, hearing someone be sweet to Beezlebub for once is nice. Everyone was always so scared of him, or squicked out by the fact that he was a moth.

I shake my head as realization slams into me. "Wait," I snort. "Luna like . . . like . . ." I can't bring myself to finish the sentence. Instead, my fingers point upward at the ceiling, my eyes trailing from the pale woman to my own fingers as if that will help me understand what's happening.

"Mhm." Luna smiles sweetly at me and Beezlebub flies off her shoulder, coming to land on mine. At least he cares enough to know I'm about to fucking pass out.

"Like the Moon?" I ask, just for clarification.

"One and the same," Luna purrs, picking at the damn near see-through material covering her body.

I shake my head, wagging my finger around as if that's going to convince the . . . the . . . is she a spirit? A Goddess? I don't know what to even call this woman. A hysterical laugh slips past my lips and Beezlebub rubs his fuzzy face against my neck.

"I summoned the Moon," I mumble to no one in particular between laughs. "Oh, Goddess."

At least she's hot.

Chapter 4
Luna

Licking my lips, I hum along to the Elysium songs drifting on the wind. Every once in a while, the sound of a prayer, a bit of a spell, the sound of joy or pain will reach my ears, fragments from the mortal realm. Their attention feeds this plane, it nourishes all the beauty around me.

I stoop to swipe my finger over a moon blossom and pause as an unfamiliar tingling sensation creeps up my body. It begins in my toes and in my panic, I think lifting my feet from the ground will stop it. Even as I hover above the lavender grass, the bone deep sensation winds further up my body until it reaches my neck. My heart pounds against my chest.

"What's happening?" I cry out, but there's no one around to hear me. I have no consort to save me from whatever's happening, no lover to console me, even if they don't know what's happening, no friends to stand by me as my heart feels like it might burst into flame.

> "We welcome you into your nights,
> To bless us, guard us, until the return of light."

A SWEET, TINKLING VOICE CHANTS THE WORDS. SHE SAYS SOMETHING else, but her voice fades in and out like she's moving away from me. I try to turn my head, instinctively chasing the sound but my body won't obey me. My muscles tense, shaking under the exertion as I try my best to move. I'd settle even for the tiniest movement at this point.

As I struggle against the invisible force binding me, my vision swims. The moon blossoms swirl and fade before me. Their silver petals float far away from my reach. Even the lavender grass they're nestled in blurs and eventually vanishes. The world becomes one unbreakable swirl of color. My fingers dance across the vivid hues as my body is ripped from my home and thrown through a portal.

I can at least move now.

That should be comforting, but it's not. I'm the Moon, for creation's sake. Something as arbitrary as moving my fingers through the interdimensional ether shouldn't feel like a victory. I was present when the Great Goddess birthed the ether. I narrow my eyes in indignation as I watch the colorful show dissipate, as my feet plant themselves firmly onto the ground.

The first thing to bombard my senses is the smell. Nowhere in Creation smells this badly, surely. I wave my hands around trying to clear the air and quickly realize I'm surrounded by a dense fog. No, smoke. I'm surrounded by a dense, blue tinted smoke. It burns my nostrils and my eyes water as I focus on clearing the smoke.

I have no idea where I am, but apparently it's on fire. Fantastic. Inhaling a deep breath of smoke-filled air, I raise my hand to summon a door to my home realm. As I press against the air to unlock the ether, my palm is zapped by some kind of invisible barrier. I shake my hand out, annoyed by the minor twinge of pain, and focus all of my attention on the task at hand. I envision the ether opening, creating a door for me to walk through. Still, nothing but a small arc of electricity greets me where the portal should be forming.

Twirling a finger in agitation, I swirl the smoke away from me. Some sort of winged creature flies by my head and I turn, trying to keep an eye on it in the dissipating smoke. If I can't get home, I need to make wherever I am as safe and comfortable as possible. Just until I can figure out why my magic isn't working properly. The jarring sound of someone coughing brings my eyes to the woman standing by the open door.

Her long, platinum blonde hair tumbles down her shoulders as she coughs into her hand. It's obvious the moment she notices me. Her pale, freckled cheeks blush a deeper shade of pink as her hand covers her chest.

"Who the fuck are you?" she yelps, her chest rising and falling quickly as her eyes scan the room and then settle back on me. My skin tingles under her attention as she looks me over.

So, we're on Earth then. That means the woman who summoned me must be a witch. I cock an eyebrow and watch each emotion pass over the startled girl. Panic. Confusion. Interest. Apprehension.

"Who-who are you, hot stuff?" She pushes a stray piece of wavy hair behind her ear and I realize her hair isn't quite platinum. It's more of an ombre of varying shades of grey, silver, and blonde. "How'd you get in here?"

Why is she asking me these questions? She's obviously the one who summoned me. I spin in a slow circle, taking in the altar, the small cauldron still spitting wisps of blue smoke into the air, the Yule log leaned against the window. "I'm Luna," I whisper without thinking as I study the strange furnishings in the room. The seating seems to be raised off the ground and there's a black mirror on the wall with a small red light in the corner.

It must be the witches' new way of communicating with one another. They have always loved their mirror magic.

"Luna who? How the hell did you get in here?" Her tone is sharp, bringing me to a stop. I level her with a severe glare, her icy blue eyes meeting my own.

"Mortals sure are surlier than I remember."

"Excuse me?"

The winged creature swoops down in front of me and this time I'm finally able to see what it is. The large, beautifully patterned moth lights atop my shoulder and I coo to him.

"Hello!" I brush a finger across his fuzzy little back and sigh as a rush of magic swirls across my skin. He's her familiar. The giant moth floods me with a sense of protectiveness and I grin at him. I have no intention of harming his witch. She isn't powerful enough to do me harm.

I can't help but wonder what transpired to bring me here, though. Her magic is weak compared to the witches of the past. Maybe she's a hybrid of some kind, a human witch. The moth prattles away at me, a sweet vibrating sound that comes from his too-large mouth. No, while it's true that witches were responsible for the death of Orion, and forced Celestials from this realm, it's clear to me this witch isn't a threat.

"Wait," she laughs from her place by the door. "Luna like . . . like . . ." she waves her finger in a ridiculous circle, pointing upward. A laugh tries to bubble past my lips but I swallow it with a smile and nod.

"Mhm." The familiar lifts off from my shoulder and flies to his witch, nestling against her shoulder. This is a strange witch, indeed. Her shock seems genuine and I can't help but wonder why she summoned me.

"Like the Moon?"

"One and the same." I smooth my hands down my dress, trying to be patient with the flighty woman. She summoned me here and doesn't seem to want to take responsibility for it. Is she scared of me? What sort of a witch fears the Moon?

Before I can ask, a round of hysterical giggles erupts from the girl. She waves her finger around, as if admonishing me, and I take a step back.

"What do you think—"

"I summoned the Moon," she laughs. "Oh, Goddess."

I've had about enough of the eccentric woman and try again to summon a doorway to my realm. The magic in my fingers reflects off the air, completely missing the ether, and shoots back into my palm again. It burns more this time and I shake my hand, glaring at my captor.

"You'd dare to trap me here?" I ask, holding her gaze.

"I didn't even bring you here," she yelps, her eyes going wide. "Or, I didn't mean to." Her anxiety is palpable, like a shimmer glinting off her skin.

"Yes you did, your voice was as clear as moonlight," I sigh. "We welcome you into our nights, to bless us, guard us, until the return of light." I rush through the words, rolling my eyes at the ending phrase.

Those are the words keeping me here, I'm almost certain of it. *Until the return of light.* Swallowing a groan, I run my fingers through my hair and wait to hear her response.

"Oh shit," she squeaks, closing the door firmly and sliding to the ground. "This is real. Okay, well, um—" she scratches her head just behind her ear, obviously panicking.

Any reservations I had about whether or not she is a danger are put to rest as I watch her have a panic attack in the floor. The moth rubs his furry face against her neck, chittering nonsense I can barely hear from this distance.

"Who are *you*? You didn't mean to summon me?" My nose wrinkles as I'm once again faced with the fact that I have no control in this situation. I've never enjoyed losing control and probably never will. If eons hadn't changed that, one sad witch definitely wouldn't.

"I'm Alandra," she hiccups, pressing a hand against her forehead. "Alandra Michaels. And no, I didn't mean to bring you here, obviously."

I hum noncommittally, closing my eyes for a brief moment to sense the magic around us. *Alandra,* as she calls herself, is barely a blip on the map in my mind. Surrounding us on all sides, however, are blips of varying strength and severity. One particularly strong pulse of magic seems to be drawing closer, actually.

I've been summoned into a coven. Every nerve in my body catches fire under the anxiety that brings me. I'd felt all the pain, every piece of misery that passed through his being when Orion died, just like every other Celestial. We have always been connected on a deep level.

She may not be a threat, but the rest of them . . .

I open my mouth to tell her as much when a strange roar sounds somewhere outside the house.

"What is that?" I ask, as light shines in through the window, illuminating the room. Shielding my eyes with my hand, I try to focus on what's happening outside the window.

"Fuck!" Alandra hisses, crossing the room and grabbing my hand. A small gasp slips past my lips when her soft fingers wrap around mine and she pulls me down the dark hall. "My sister is home. She can't know you're here. Not until we figure this out. Please?" She opens the door to a smaller room, and I step inside, staring down at our entwined fingers before I raise my eyes to her face again. That *'please'* is hard to ignore.

I pull my fingers from hers and nod my head solemnly. Alandra flashes me an apologetic grin and quickly closes the door behind her. I stand there for a moment, softly brushing my fingertips over the places where our skin had touched.

How long has it been since I felt the touch of another being? The Celestials only gather during alignments, and when was the last time that happened? Shaking my head, I press my ear to the door, trying to listen to whatever is happening out there.

"What in creation?" Listening so hard I nearly strain my ears, the tiny pulse of magic in the house brushes against my mind and I realize what's happening. They've soundproofed the rooms.

Clever witches.

With the flick of a finger, I bring down the soundproofing, and eavesdrop on the conversation in the hall.

"Oh wow, you must have done a really good job with the spell!" a cheery voice exclaims.

"Yeah?" Alandra sounds nervous, self-conscious even. My hand lays across the hollow of my throat. I should feel guilty for intruding, but to be fair, I was sort of just kidnapped. Even if it was an accident.

"Yeah, girl. As soon as I walked in the house, I could feel a new zip of power. Good job, Bug!"

I shake my head, roll my eyes, and throw myself onto the plushy bed in the back of the room. This bedchamber is set up strangely, in my opinion. There's no fountain. And where does she keep her food? Contemplating the travesty of that, I flip the soundproofing back on, just to be safe.

The little witch doesn't want her sister to know I'm here. I'll respect that until I can't anymore. I've never had a sister, but my relationship with the other Celestials has always been complicated—especially with the sun. He is incorrigible. Everything is a competition with him. If I touch it, he has to also touch it, and undo all my beautiful work. I imagine having a sibling to be something like that.

The door creaks open and I lift my head, my hand flicking up reflexively.

"It's just me," Alandra hisses over the soft click of the door closing. Another click rings out in the quiet of the room. Bracing myself on my elbow, I cross my legs and watch as Alandra hesitates at the edge of the room. She's staring at me like she expects something.

I raise my eyebrow in challenge. *I know she doesn't expect me to sleep on the floor.* With a huff, the young witch crosses the room and grabs a pillow from the other side of the bed, tossing it down on the floor.

I grin to myself as I let my head fall back on the pillow, staring out the window at the night sky. *Small victories.*

Chapter 5

Alandra

I squish the pillow under my head, trying to fluff it up enough to pretend the floor is comfortable and huff. Beezlebub chitters on the wall behind my head and I flip him off.

"Don't be sarcastic," I mutter.

"Excuse me?" Luna asks from the bed.

I freeze, my heart rate speeding up again. The sound of the woman's voice is beyond melodic. It's like the fairy music they warn little children not to follow into the woods, disarming, alarming, and alluring all once. I swallow my instincts and shut my eyes before I answer.

"Not you ... ma'am ... I was talking to Beezlebub." Do you call the Moon 'ma'am'? I really have no idea how to handle this social situation. I'm not a fan of social interaction in the first place. My favorite hoodie even reads: A large gathering of people is called a nope. Words to live by.

The snort from the bed doesn't sound very immortally-graceful-being-like to me, but who am I to judge?

"Luna is fine. You named your familiar Beelzebub?" The bed squeaks under her weight and I'm sure if I open my eyes, I'll see her peering down at me from the bed, but I'm just not ready to deal with that at the moment.

"No, not Beelzebub. Beezlebub."

"What in creation is the difference?"

One eye pops open and I find myself staring up at Luna, just like I thought. Her white-blonde hair hangs around her face like a curtain while she peers down at me. I wish I had a name for the color of her eyes, but blue or silver just doesn't seem to do the hue justice. They're like frozen silver. Winterized metal. I chew my lip as I realize the heavy eye contact is probably disrespectful and glance away.

"Well," I sigh, trying to clear my head. It's hard to think with her staring at me like that. Her porcelain skin glows in the darkness, just enough to see her clearly. The fucking Moon, I groan internally. What have you done this time, Alandra? Ignoring the sound of my subconscious self-deprecation, I explain B's name. "Beelzebub, as I'm sure you know, is the name of a very specific, nasty demon. I wouldn't name my familiar after him, in case speaking his name that often gave him a foothold in my home. Beezlebub though," I enunciate his name carefully, focusing on the subtle difference in pronunciation. "It matched B's personality without making my mom uncomfortable."

"That's ridiculous," Luna laughs. "It's the same name."

"It isn't," I groan. "Go to bed."

"Are you bossing me around, Little Witch?" Her voice isn't severe but a pang of anxiety still sears my poor brain. What a damn day. I summoned the moon. The Moon is laying in my bed. And she has a smart ass mouth. Can I get an attitude with her? Will she smite me?

"Yes." I decide it's easier to treat her like any other annoying woman in my life. "Go to sleep. You stole the bed, you might as well use it."

As I shimmy against my pillow again, trying to get comfortable, the bed squeaks and groans. "I'm not a thief." Luna shifts again, sending the bed into another fit of rage.

I roll my eyes, trying to embrace the silence, but Luna's annoyance permeates everything in the room.

"What is it like being a Celestial? Is there something specific I should call you?"

"Luna is fine. Being a Celestial is just like being a witch, I think," she laughs. "Humans think you feel different than they do, yes?"

"I guess so."

"But you're not so different. What's normal for you is just different than their normal, that's all. It's the same for Celestials and witches."

I blink up at the ceiling, contemplating that. She has a point. Jess had asked me on multiple occasions what being a witch was like and I never really had an answer for her. Then again, I thought it might be due to me being the world's worst witch.

"I'm sorry. I don't know if I apologized before, but I am sorry. I didn't mean to bring you here and I don't know why you can't get home. We'll fix it, I promise."

"I have no doubts, Alandra," Luna whispers. Hearing her say my name does unseemly things to my insides. My stomach clenches, the skin tensing underneath my flat palm. She oozes power. Even I can feel it rolling off of her in waves and I've never been hyper-sensitive to magic before. Everything she says—even the sassy comments—seems to drip with power.

Now that the initial shock is wearing off, and the fact that a Celestial being is lying in my bedroom is sinking in, I'm faced with a healthy dose of fear. I know she could probably snap me out of existence if she wanted to.

"Your unease is unsettling me, please stop worrying over whatever it is."

"Oh, right, sorry." She's an empath? Pulling the thin blanket up under my chin, I try to focus on anything other than the fact that I've probably pissed off the most powerful being I'll ever meet. "What's the Celestial realm like?"

"Well, there isn't one Celestial realm, there's one for each of us. We each have to manage our portion of creation. You sound really uncomfortable down there, just come up here, already."

I blink, swallowing slowly. "What?"

"Just come lay in your bed, I promise I won't bite." Is that sarcasm? Even though it's ridiculous, I cringe as thoughts of all the people sacrificed to the Celestials over the eons flash through my mind. Maybe she does bite.

"Uh, okay," I mumble, grabbing my pillow. As I sit up, I notice that Luna is already on the opposite end of the bed, laying on her side. Everything about her exudes confidence, but I suppose if I was a Celestial, I'd be confident, too. She's absolutely comfortable, her head lounging gracefully across the side of her arm, her other hand cupping her smooth hip where it rises away from her torso. Letting out a breath, I crawl onto the bed, placing the pillow how I want it.

"There, now," Luna murmurs. "My home is beautiful, that's what you wanted to know, yes?"

"What's it like there?"

"It's colorful but muted. The world is different than what you're accustomed to, I think, unless Earth has changed unimaginably in the past few thousand years." She squirms down into the bed between sentences, letting out a heavy breath. "The grass grows purple there, a beautiful light shade of lavender that compliments the night sky. Moon blossoms grow everywhere, on everything. You'd think of them like a weed, but they're too beautiful to contemplate removing. Music from Elysium drifts in and out of ear shot, the prayers and spells of mortals do the same. It's eternally night, but not dark. I don't know how to explain it, really." She sounds entranced, like she misses home already.

"It sounds beautiful."

"It is, Alandra, truly. I'd say I'd show you, but we don't bring mortals into the Celestial realms anymore."

"Why not?" My nose scrunches up at her comment. Are Celestials prejudiced?

"A very long time ago, your kind betrayed mine. We still love you. We're still linked irreparably by the magic this universe sprouted from, but we've never been able to recover from that betrayal." Her face falls into a passive frown, her eyes sliding shut.

"What did we do?"

"Do they not teach you the history of your own kind?" She yawns, covering her mouth as her sleepy voice drifts between us.

"Well, I think I'd remember a story about our entire race pissing off another entire race. Our problematic history with humans hasn't been hidden—"

"Were you a good student?" Luna asks, an amused smile quirking her lips.

"No."

"I didn't think so."

I roll over to my other side, facing away from Luna, and pull the blanket up over my shoulder. The house isn't drafty but something about knowing it's cold outside makes me want to snuggle into a cocoon of blankets and disappear until spring. It always has.

The sound of soft, even breaths breaks up the silence in the room and I smile to myself. The Moon sleeps, how cute. There's a lot I don't know about the Celestials, apparently. I wonder if other witches my age realize they're like actual people, with bodies. Gorgeous bodies.

As my mind stumbles over that pervasive thought, a slender arm snakes around my waist and a new warmth presses against my back. I freeze, unsure of how to react.

Luna lets out a tiny sigh, the most adorable fucking sound I've ever heard and I close my eyes. She's still asleep. The Moon sleeps and likes to snuggle. A smile tugs at my lips as I chase the darkness behind my lids.

My fingers graze the top of the tall, billowing, lavender grass. It tickles my thighs as I walk across an empty plain. Every few feet, a silver flower stands proud, glistening in the glowing atmosphere.

There's no light in the sky above me. No sun. No moon. Millions of stars twinkle brighter than I've ever noticed before and my chest races as I reach out for them, wondering if I can touch one. What looks like glitter rains down from the sky when my fingers brush against the twinkling black night. I brush the strange substance from my shoulder and laugh.

"Stardust," a familiar voice calls out.

My head swivels around as I search for the source of the voice but find no one. It's just me and the stars. I take another step through the grass, looking for something. I want to find . . . what do I want to find?

A trilling voice sings an ancient song, wavering in and out of existence like the signal on an old radio. I find myself running after the music, trying to find the source, but every time I think I've got it, it fades away again.

"Where are you?" I ask. My own voice sounds odd, quieter than normal. Holding my hand up in front of my face, spread my fingers and gasp at the faint glow coming from them. It's almost like—

"Moonlight."

"Who's there?" I spin in a circle, searching for whoever is speaking to me

but find no one. Faint laughter echoes in the distance and I run toward it, smiling. This feels like a game. Like I'm a child and my playmate is just over the hill ahead of me.

As I speed through the tall grass, tiny fireflies fly up from their hiding spot, blinking as they flit around me. Happiness bubbles in my throat and I take off again, cresting the hill. The vision below me takes my breath away.

Where I'd expected the lavender plain to stretch on forever, a large palace made of almost see-through white rock stands on a flat ground in the middle of a teal lake.

"So beautiful," I murmur, taking a step toward the island home.

My eyes blink open slowly and I roll onto my back. Luna's arm drapes across my stomach with her face smushed into my shoulder. That can't be comfortable. With a yawn, I stretch my arms over my head and she rolls away from me, mumbling something in her sleep.

A knock sounds at the door and I jerk upright, my heart racing. I glance from the door to Luna and cringe. Laney is going to lose her shit if I don't get this woman home today and finds out about her.

"Fuck me," I growl, throwing my legs over the edge of the bed. I want to ask Luna be quiet, but I also don't want to wake her. I rush to the door and crack it open, looking at my sister with bleary eyes.

"What's up?" I ask, leaning into the open space of the door.

"What are you doing?" Laney asks, her nose scrunching up as she stares up at me. She presses against the door and I panic, holding it firmly in place.

"I was sleeping until someone woke me up," I snap.

"I just wanted to let you know I'm leaving. I have to go to work with the kids in town today. I wanted to see if you need anything but if you're going to be a bi—"

A soft sound comes from the room behind me and Laney's eyes light up. "Ooooh, do you have a girl in there? Who is it?" She stands on her tippy toes, trying to peer around me and I roll my eyes, pushing the door a little more closed.

"Shhh, go be great," I whisper.

"Love you, Bug!"

"Love you too, now gooooo." I close the door quickly and press my back to it, blowing out a heavy breath.

"Is she gone?" a soft voice calls from the bed.

My eyes track Beezlebub flitting across the room. He lands on the window, his front feet raising to tap on the window. Intellectually, I know it doesn't make a sound, but in my mind I can hear the subtle *tap, tap, tap* from across the room. I roll my eyes. He loves to go out exploring, but that's not happening right now. Right now, I just want to hide in this room until Laney is a safe distance away.

"She's leaving for work." My fingers rake through my hair as I take in the woman lying across my bed. Her pale skin wrapped in my white sheets is enticing as fuck, I have to admit. I know her dress is still intact beneath those sheets, but my mind doesn't seem to care.

"Now what?" she asks, snapping me out of my momentary fantasy.

"Ugh, fuck." I press my palm to my forehead and groan. I have a million things I need to be doing. I did *not* ask for this. "I guess we need to figure out how to get you home."

"What do you need from me?"

I want to be honest with her, to explain I'm really a terrible witch, and I probably will not be able to fix this, but I don't want to admit my inadequacy to her. I don't want her to see me in the same light everyone else does. Useless. Practically a null.

"Can you walk me through how you usually get from realm to realm? Maybe something in the spell—"

Luna waves her hand, cutting me off, and then flattens her palm as if she's pushing against a wall. Her eyebrows draw down low on her face and I take a step toward the bed, curious. The power in the room shifts around us. It's obvious she's using magic, but I don't see any physical result. After a moment, Luna draws her hand back with a yelp and begins shaking it.

"Since I arrived here, this is what happens," she grumbles. "The rest of my powers seem to be intact, but I can't access the ether."

"Hmm." I take another step toward the bed, coming to a stop at the edge and hold out my hand. "Let me see."

She obliges, placing her hand in mine, palm up. My fingertips trace over the lines in her palm, brushing against the sizzling after-effects of her magic.

"Somehow my power has been bound." Luna pulls her hand from mine slowly, her eyes trailing up to meet mine. "I think it has to do with how you worded your spell."

"What? No way, I read it word for word."

"Show it to me."

I cross the room to the door and hold up a finger, signaling for her to wait, and open the door. Rushing out into the hall, I slide into the living room and call out for Laney.

"You here?" I ask. No answer. Making my way to the window, I hesitate in front of the altar where everything from the blessing still lays. A quick glance out the window reveals her car is gone.

"Come on out," I call out loudly, hoping Luna will hear me. I sink to my knees in front of the altar and grab the piece of paper to read it. I skim the words, searching for what could have possibly went wrong. It all sounds normal to me, but what do I know? My teeth scrape over my bottom lip as I look at the carefully crafted spellwork. It's meant to be a run of the mill blessing, not a summoning spell. And it definitely wasn't meant to trap Luna in this realm.

"Find anything?" Luna asks as she sits down beside me.

"Not really, but maybe you should look." I hand her the spell and watch as her eyes track back and forth across the paper until they pause on a certain spot. I'm not entirely sure if a Celestial would understand spellwork or not, but it can't hurt to try.

"It reads like a Yule blessing," she scoffs. "But what is this list at the bottom?" She turns the paper around and points to the small list of herbs I was meant to gather from the herbalist.

"Ah, we were out of those and I was supposed to—"

"Supposed?"

"Well, the herbalist was closed already so I substituted some things." I cringe, realizing where this is going.

"What did you use instead of cardamom and cedar?" Luna's fingers hold tight to the paper. It's obvious she's annoyed.

"Chickweed and calamus," I whisper, flinching when she lets out a loud huff.

"Well no wonder," she snaps. "The way the spell is worded, with those ingredients . . . it's a summoning. It would have been fine if you left them off completely, or *used the right ingredients!*"

"Don't yell at me. I don't need this shit right now either, okay?" Dragging my hands down my face, I groan. "How do we fix it?"

"I don't know. The way the spell is worded it seems like you've summoned me here until the solstice."

"Oh Goddess," I whisper, my pulse ringing in my ears. "I can't hide you from Laney for that long."

"That's what you're worried about?" Her nostrils flare and the ends of her hair seem to lift of their own accord, but I know better. She's gathering power, likely without even realizing it. I've seen it before with Laney. Luna's chest rises and falls rapidly with angry breaths. Her cheeks flush pink as her eyes flash a dangerous silver, completely devoid of the wintery blue hue that caught my attention before.

"No!" I squeak. "I know you're stuck here and that's a terrible inconvenience and I'm sorry. I just—I just don't know how to fix it. I'm sorry. I'm trying here, okay?"

Luna takes a deep breath, her eyes falling shut as she tries to calm herself. The power flowing through her dissipates and her hair floats down around her shoulders where it belongs. Letting out an uneasy breath, I try to remember anything I've learned that could help here.

"A banishing spell might work?" I pose it as a question because I'm honestly not sure.

"If it did, you'd regret it. Banishing me could prevent you from accessing moon magic for the rest of your life. Is that something you're willing to risk?" Luna inclines her head to the side, obviously intrigued by the thought.

"I mean," I sigh. "I did this and it's not fair to you. I'd just have to deal with it." A knot forms in my stomach. Moon magic is one of the few things I enjoy casting. I make a wonderful tea from moon water that helps with creative blocks.

"Interesting," she purrs. "I'm going to bathe. The room with the toilet is the right one, yes?"

I snort, nodding as she stands up. "Make sure you test the water with your hand first, I don't want you to get burned."

"Why would it burn me?" Luna's eyes go wide as if it's the most terrifying thing she's ever heard.

"The water is heated, if you turn it up too high it could hurt."

"Modern convenience," she laughs. "How interesting."

I shake my head as I watch her practically glide out of the room and down the hallway. This should be interesting.

LUNA STARES AT THE SANDWICH ON HER PLATE EVEN AS I BITE INTO MY own. Ham, cheese, mayo, mustard, and the tiniest bit of hot sauce... it's the best sandwich ever, but she doesn't seem very impressed.

"Is there something wrong?" I sit my sandwich down and grab a napkin, wiping the tiny breadcrumbs from my hands. She didn't eat dinner last night, hadn't asked for breakfast this morning, and now it seems like she's going to pass on lunch as well. Do Celestials not eat?

Luna bites her bottom lip, her eyes never leaving the plate before her. Her hand slides over her throat to the back of her neck. "Well," she finally begins. "This just isn't quite what I'm used to."

"Do Celestials not eat?" I ask aloud this time. It's not like I know a lot about her kind. Maybe she exists solely on moonlight. Maybe she eats magic or something, hell, I don't know.

"No, we do. It's just—" Luna lets out a dramatic sigh. "I mostly eat moon blossoms. I've never stayed in this realm long enough to eat your food before." Her eyes rise to meet mine and I snort.

"Well, we don't have moon blossoms. But what I heard is you're a vegetarian and luckily for you," I murmur as I slide the seat out from the kitchen table. "My ex-girlfriend was a vegetarian. Let me see if I can't make you something you'd like better."

Luna grimaces and pushes the plate away. "Thank the Great Goddess."

I roll my eyes and turn toward the fridge, opening it to see what we have that a veggie might like. Jess ate a lot of pasta, but if Luna preferred flowers...

"A salad might be more up your alley," I reason, picking through the fridge for a bag of lettuce and a few extra ingredients. Laying everything out on the sink, I pull a knife from the wooden block and begin chopping a tomato.

"That looks really—" Luna's head snaps to the side, her attention solely on the door.

"What's wrong?"

"I think your sister is here," she murmurs, pushing the chair out.

"Shit," I whisper, laying the knife down on the counter. "Okay." I blow out a long breath and quickly toss all the ingredients into a bowl for Luna. Hopefully, the salad would be easier for her to eat. Even if she has to eat it in seclusion.

Luna holds my gaze for a moment, confusion etched across her face. "Do you want me to go back to your bedchamber?"

"What? It's a bedroom and no," I groan, handing her the bowl of salad. "I can't hide you forever. She's going to find out, unfortunately. Maybe she can help."

"Is she trustworthy? Your sister?'

"Yeah, I'd say so. What do you mean, though?"

Luna looks cautiously toward the door and then back down at the food in her hands. I can tell something's bothering her, but I'm not sure what. As powerful as she is, why would she be afraid of Laney? Don't get me wrong, my sister is a total fucking bad ass and *I* would be afraid of her . . . but I'm also not an immortal being with insane amounts of magic at my fingertips.

"Forget it," Luna sighs, taking the bowl to the table. I reach into the fridge and grab a bottle of dressing—French, the absolute best—and set it on the table beside her.

"This makes it tastier, at least for me."

The door beings to creak open and an entirely new wave of panic washes through me. My eyes go wide as my pulse thrums in my eardrums. "Change of plans," I whisper, shooing Luna toward the pantry in the back of the dining room.

"I thought you wanted me to—"

"Shh, quiet, please," I beg as I open the door, waiting for her to step inside.

Luna narrows her eyes on me, her knuckles turning white as I step into the pantry. She opens her mouth to say something but I quickly shut the door, turning around just in time to see Laney pop out from behind the front door.

"Hey, Bug," she calls out in a cheery voice but her face quickly changes into an expression of worry. "What's wrong?"

"Nothing." I step away from the door, narrowing my eyes on Beezlebub as he flies over my head to perch on it. *Traitor.*

"Mmmhm," she muses as she makes her way to the dining room table. Her eyes fall to what appears to be a random bottle of French dressing. "Why didn't you put this up when you were done eating?"

"Lazy, I guess," I laugh nervously. I'm a better liar than this, normally. But I'm not used to having to lie to *Laney.*

"You're being weird, what's wrong?" Laney walks hesitantly into the kitchen and grabs a bottle of fizzy water from the fridge. "Did something happen?"

"Like what?" I ask innocently.

"The way you're acting, I'm tempted to ask if you burnt the house down. Luckily, I can see it's still standing. What did you do?" She takes a sip of the water, her eyes never leaving mine.

I shrug nonchalantly. I don't have a good lie ready and it's better to let her fill in the blanks herself than to come up with something too outlandish.

"Did you and Mom get into it again?"

"N—Yes," I sigh. "She reached out, I didn't respond. So I guess we kinda are still in it, at the moment."

"Bug," Laney groans. "She's our *Mom.* You have to forgive her."

"Why do you always expect me to forgive them for being horrible to me?" I snap. "I get they're perfect parents to you, but they're fucking ridiculous to me. I've never done anything except try to be happy with who I am and they treat me like utter shit for it, Laney." I hadn't planned on committing to this cover story quite so hard but for Goddess' sake, she always defends them no matter what they do to me. I'm tired of it.

"You're right." Laney sets the water down on the counter and braces herself against the edge. "I'm sorry."

"Come again?"

"I'm not repeating it," she laughs. "But yeah, I get it. What she said was fucked up. I'll stay out of it."

My eyebrows shoot up my forehead in shock and Laney shakes her head.

"For now!" she adds. "If you and Mom haven't made up before we go for Yule, I'm putting you in timeout."

A quiet *crunch* comes from somewhere nearby and I quickly busy myself with putting the dressing back in the fridge.

Laney crosses her arms, turning to rest her hip against the counter.

Crunch.

"Alandra," she chides. "What was that?"

Crrrrrrrunch.

"What was what?" I ask, trying my best to look puzzled.

"What's going on?" she asks again, frustration building in her tone. Beezlebub chitters away from his perch on the door and Laney cocks an eyebrow before taking a step toward the pantry.

"Wait!" I rush out, groaning when a smile splits her face.

"Bug . . . what's in the pantry?"

"Nothing! Why would anything be in there?"

"Bug." She narrows her eyes, trying to take another step toward toward Luna's hiding spot but I quickly maneuver in front of her.

"It's a raccoon!" I blurt out.

"A raccoon?" Laney rolls her eyes. "Why would you put a raccoon in the pantry?"

"I uh—I left the back door open and it snuck in, I guess. I came out to find it chowing down on my chips on the table, so I shooed it into the pantry. I panicked."

"You shooed a raccoon—who had already eaten some of our food—into a closet full of more of our food?" Laney's face breaks out into another smile as I nod. "I put a protection spell around the house to keep out pests when we moved in, remember?"

Shit.

Laney laughs as she pushes past me and twists open the pantry door. In the middle of the small room, Luna sits on her knees, a bag of chips in one hand, a chip close to her mouth in the other. Her eyes go wide as she looks up toward Laney.

"Hello," she murmurs, climbing to her feet slowly. The half eaten bowl of salad sits on the floor, abandoned for the bag of kettle cooked potato chips.

"Hiiiii," Laney drawls out before turning to me. *"Is this her?"* she mouths as Luna sweeps past her, chips and bowl of salad in hand, toward the dining room table.

I shrug, unsure of what to say or do.

"Eeeeep!" she squeals, then half jogs over to the table to introduce herself. "I'm Laney, Bug's sister. It's so nice to meet you!" Laney holds out her hand and Luna looks from me to her, suspiciously, before finally taking it in her own.

Laney pulls her hand back with a gasp. "Holy shit. Where did you find her? That's some serious magic!" She shakes her hand out and takes a seat at the table, slowly unwrapping the scarf from around her neck.

"I uh—" I really don't want to *lie* to her. I know she's going to find out.

"We just met," Luna interjects. It's the truth, at least.

"Well, Mom and Dad are going to *love* this," Laney coos.

"Love what?" Luna asks, her eyebrows furrowing together.

Laney giggles and I groan. *Fuck.* I really shouldn't have let her think that I had *that* kind of company earlier. This is going to get super awkward super fast and there's nothing I can really do about it at this point.

"Well, you know, with Bug being a little magically challenged and all—"

"Laney!" I snap. My cheeks heat under the no doubt singeing red blush that's creeping across them.

"I just mean they'll be happy, especially considering your last girlfriend was human. That's all." She shrugs and begins wringing her scarf in her hands. I know she didn't mean to embarrass me, but holy fuck, who does that?

"Girlfriend?" Luna lays a hand on her chest and laughs and I feel the blush creep farther down my cheeks. "Oh. I'm not—well, you see —we just met." Luna grabs the bottle of French dressing from the table, pours more onto her salad, and picks up her fork, as if dismissing the conversation.

"Ohhhh," Laney sings with a goofy grin. "Far be it for me to judge. We all go through our whoring phase."

"*What?*" Luna asks and my heart pounds against my chest as her hair begins to swirl. Her magic feels like all the air is being sucked from the room as it rushes toward her, feeding her, feeding the power that grows inside her with every word she speaks. "I'm not a *whore*," she growls.

Laney's eyes go wide and she backs away from the table. She hasn't even raised a hand defensively. Something in her probably recognizes that she'd lose the fight. Her fire magic is fucking brutal . . . but the kind of energy Luna is throwing off would scare anyone away. Anyone except me, apparently.

I lay a hand on her shoulder. "She didn't mean offense."

"I really didn't. Bug, who is this?" Laney crosses her arms and Luna goes back to her salad, taking a big bite of the soggy greens covered in too much French dressing.

"Well," I begin, taking a step around the side of the table toward my sister. She's going to lose her shit and I know it. "I may have accidentally summoned her last night."

"Summoned? What do you mean? I checked the altar before I went to bed and the only spellwork was for the Moon blessing—" Laney's eyes go wider. I didn't think that was possible, to be honest. "Holy fuck! Alandra Michaels, did you summon the Moon? Into our house?" Laney's voice gets higher with each word she speaks and I find myself cringing and taking a step back.

"It wasn't on purpose," I point out quickly before taking another step behind Luna. The original plan was to be between them when this realization hit. But now, I'm reconsidering that. At least if I'm behind the big bad Moon spirit—Celestial, whatever—Laney won't try to throw any magic at me. I've lost a few good hoodies to her fuckery in the past and this seems like one of those occasions.

Chapter 6
Alandra

"OH MY GODS AND GODDESSES!" she yells, pointing at me. "What did you do?"

Luna visibly tenses and cocks her head to the side. My gaze slides from my sister to the Celestial at our dinner table and I swallow hard.

"I accidentally summoned the Moon," I admit. "But before you yell, I don't think she likes it. I'm going to be totally honest, sis, maybe you should chill out a bit before you—"

"She's not a goddamn chihuahua! She isn't going to pee herself because one of *us* raises our voice. Do you know what she is? Do you know what she can do?"

"Do you?" Luna asks on a deadly whisper.

"Laney—"

"Sorry." Laney's face pales all except two bright red spots on both her cheeks. She's always turned red when she was mad. This is beyond the norm though. "How do we send her home?" She focuses her attention on Luna, taking a long, deep breath. "I'm so sorry this has happened, we are going to fix it immediately. We'll get you home. Please don't, uh, curse us or anything."

Luna snorts and I roll my eyes.

"It's not funny, Bug."

"Well, it's a little funny. You have polka dots on your cheeks because you're pissed off but you're terrified so you're also as pale as a damned ghost. Stop yelling at me and tell me how to fix it. I thought I could do it on my own and was wrong." I wrap my arms around my stomach, thankful for the baggy hoodie I'm still wearing.

"I don't curse people, either," Luna points out. "I truly believe your sister didn't mean to bring me here and I don't think she means me any harm. You, however, have both the power and the aptitude to put me in danger. Should I be concerned?"

"What?" Laney and I both ask at the same time. Realization flashes in Laney's eyes and she shakes her head back and forth quickly.

"I would never. I'd like to say witches have evolved past that, but I can't speak for everyone else in the witching world, only for myself. I'd never harm a Celestial." Laney looks almost embarrassed, her cheeks flushing brighter as she rushes through the overly formal statement.

"What do you mean? What does she mean?" I look from Luna to Laney, my brows furrowing in confusion.

"Don't you remember why the Celestials cut us off?" Laney asks with a huff. I take a second, trying to recount the hours and hours of magical history we'd been forced to endure as children and teenagers.

"Not particularly," I admit.

Laney leans across the table, bracing herself on her forearms. "During the Golden Age, there was a group of powerful witches. Our kind were still super connected to the Celestials, entire covens were bound to them. These particular witches didn't think that was enough power, though. They wanted more. Ringing any bells?"

I nod as she speaks. It does sound familiar.

"They thought they could access the Celestials' immortality if they sacrificed them. So they lured a Celestial into a circle and sacrificed him. At least," Laney pauses, her eyes flicking to Luna. "That's what we were taught in school."

Pouring myself into a seat, I lean back against the hardback of the chair and shake my head. I do remember the story, now that Laney mentioned it. I never put much stock into the fairytales we grew up on, though. It all sounded too convenient, but to be fair, I didn't put much stock in mythology or lore in general until Luna showed up in my living room.

I'm a very tolerant person and think people can believe whatever they choose to. If you think some guy is sitting on a cloud, judging every choice you make, go for it. If you think there are literal Gods and Goddesses flying around the world, intervening in people's lives, go right ahead. The Church of the Flying Spaghetti Monster has always been my personal favorite.

Laney knows this; she's asked me on more than one occasion how I can believe in magic but not divinity and I've always had the same answer: Magic is something that can be scientifically measured. The humans did studies on it in the eighties. People with fire affinities, for instance, are able to cause atoms to vibrate at a higher frequency until they create fire. It's magic, but it's also science. I mean, I believe in a higher power, vaguely. But I'm nowhere near as devoted or dedicated to that belief as most of my people.

Now, though? Everything seems to be fair game. I mean, the Moon is sitting at my dinner table.

"They sacrificed Orion for his power," Luna finally whispers. Her face is pained. I wonder if she was close to this Orion. "I felt it, just like every Celestial did. The things they did to him were a perversion of magic and nature. And yes, that's why Celestials turned away from this realm." Luna clears her throat, pushing the bowl of salad away from her. Apparently, the memory ruined her appetite.

"We never fully abandoned you. Each of us still receive your prayers and lend our magic to your spells. Whenever you draw on a Celestial body for your spellwork, a Celestial *allows* it. But we had to keep ourselves safe." Luna's eyes slide shut, a sad smile playing at her lips. "Death isn't natural for our kind. It was a severe loss."

My heart breaks for her. I can't imagine how loss must affect a being that's immortal. *Goddess, that's cruel.*

"I'm so sorry," I finally murmur.

Laney nods as I slide my hand across the short span of smooth tabletop to Luna's hand. Laying my palm across her fingers, I squeeze them. "We will get you home safely, I swear."

"I swear it, too," Laney adds on a whisper.

"Thank you, girls," Luna answers with a sad smile.

"I can try to do it now, if you'd like?" Laney pushes away from the table and quickly jogs across the living room to the altar. Bending to pick up the piece of paper with the spell attached, she begins walking toward us again. "Do you know what went wrong with the spell, Bug?"

With a grimace, I pull my hand away from Luna's and hide my face in my hands. "I used the wrong herbs."

A strangled sound comes from Laney and I throw my hands up in surrender. Luna shakes her head, her waves tumbling down around her face as she tries to hide her smile. Luckily, I saw it before she could dip her chin. She thinks this is funny . . .

"Make some coffee, I think this might take a while," Laney groans, shaking her head.

I shrug, pushing away from the table and head toward the coffee pot. The fact that Laney is asking for coffee instead of tea is telling; it's going to be hard as fuck to fix.

But the good news, I remind myself as I pull down the bag of coffee grounds, *is the Moon doesn't hate me and isn't going to curse my family into oblivion. That's always a plus.*

"Luna, do you drink coffee?" I ask over my shoulder.

"I've never had anything by that name. I've had tea."

"Try some coffee," Laney insists. "It's one of the best things to come out of this world, I promise you." I actually couldn't agree more. Laney doesn't drink more than a cup a day because if she gets jittery, her fire magic can be dangerous. She lost control a *few* times as a child. The rest of the times, she was just being a dick.

Behind me, Laney and Luna discuss the ins and outs of the spell-work they're crafting. Laney seems to think she can circumvent the first spell without cutting off our ties to moon magic.

"I'd never isolate a witch from the Moon," Luna whispers reverently. "I've always been honored at the connection your people feel to me. I don't want you to do anything which would jeopardize your family's ability to connect to me."

I can't help but think how fucking *sweet* that is as I move the first cup from the Keurig and begin loading creamer and sugar into it. Laney likes her coffee nearly white; it's ridiculous. I like mine a nice, medium brown.

My fingers hover near the second cup as it begins to fill. Should I make Luna's like mine or Laney's? Probably mine. I doubt she's used to refined sugars.

What a weird thought. She's a fucking Celestial, I doubt she'd have a hard time processing sugar. I shake my head and decide to load the coffee up like Laney's. At the very least, it'll taste sweet and she'll like it.

I sit the girls' cups down in front of them. "Thank you," Luna murmurs, wrapping her hands around the warm mug.

"You're welcome," I grin.

Laney tosses me a look—an accusatory look—and I turn back toward the counter, ready to make my own cup of coffee. I'm not sure what the look is about, precisely, but there's a few things to choose from. Summoning the Moon? Lying? The warm looks between myself and Luna? Behind me, a happy sigh tumbles from Luna's lips. Apparently I chose the right creamer to coffee ratio.

I take my seat between the two of them, on the side of the table, and listen to the plan.

"We should be able to use the original spellwork that was already laid out and use it to send you home." Laney points to the piece of paper she's marked all over. There's words crossed out and ingredients added to the top. Maybe it'll work, but it will be interesting regardless.

"Let's try it, Little Witch," Luna laughs. "It can't hurt." I bristle at Luna's use of the nickname for Laney. Her blazing silver eyes cut to my own, a look of question on her face. I force a smile and shrug, but the mischievous grin on Luna's face makes me think she has some inkling of the unruly emotion wreaking havoc in my stomach right now.

Why am I jealous? I barely know the woman—er, Celestial. She can call Laney whatever she wants. I just so happen to hate it a little bit for absolutely no good reason.

I disagree that it can't hurt, though. The memory of her shaking her hand when she tried to open a door to the Celestial realm in my room surges in my mind and I have to physically bite my tongue. Pain jolts through me and I nod my agreement, reluctantly.

"Okay." Laney lets out a heavy sigh and gathers up the ingredients and spellwork she's carefully plotted and walks to the altar in the living room. I follow her, coffee cup in hand and watch as she begins cleansing the area.

"This is delicious," Luna whispers near my ear. I jump, spilling a small bit of coffee on my hoodie and groan. Why am I so damn jumpy?

"I'm glad you like it," I murmur, wiping at my shirt with my sleeve, as if spreading the stain to a *different* part of my hoodie will help matters.

"Mm, I do." Luna moves more to my side and I glance at her, admiring the way her cheeks seem to have warmed since she's been here. Suddenly, I wonder if the Celestial realm is cold. I don't want to bombard her with questions, especially when Laney is working, so I keep it to myself.

Her eyes rise to meet mine and another blush works its way across my cheeks.

"Why are you embarrassed?" she asks. She hasn't broken eye contact yet. I know I probably should, since holding someone's gaze for too long can make them uncomfortable, but I'm so interested in what color her eyes actually are that I can't look away. Every time I think I have it pinned down, they seem to switch up again. Silver. Silvery blue. Almost white. It's intriguing.

"Embarrassed?" I whisper. "I'm not." That's a lie.

"Hmm," Luna muses, pressing the coffee cup to her lips again. "I'll keep that in mind. Why does she call you Bug?"

"It's my nickname." I roll my eyes. "When Beezlebub showed up as my familiar, there was a bit of an uproar with nicknaming."

"Ohhh," Luna snickers. "I can imagine. I quite like moths, though. They're rather fond of me."

"I've noticed." Even now, Beezlebub clings to the wall, almost parallel with Luna. He *is* fond of her, which is strange, because Beezlebub doesn't like anyone. Ever. Except me.

Laney lights the same candle I used during the blessing and begins murmuring the words to her spell. She drizzles some herbs into the tiny cauldron, lights them and wafts the smoke toward Luna.

"Safe travels and Blessed Be," she whispers for the final time.

I repeat her words and so does Luna, "Safe travels and Blessed Be."

The candle goes out on its own, an arc of light like lightning shoots from the tip of the wick to an empty spot beside us. The strange electricity seems to spread in the air for a moment. A small spot in the air begins to glow blue, giving way to swirling colors of all kinds.

"Oh thank Creation," Luna mutters under her breath, taking a step toward the portal. Before she can reach it, the small hole slams shut, dissipating into nothing once again. All that remains is normal, empty air.

Luna plops down firmly on her ass in the middle of the floor. Her normally beautiful, wavy hair looks like she just stuck her finger in a light socket. "Well, I don't think that worked," she grumbles, slowly standing to her feet and rubbing her hand over her bottom.

"Fuck!" My fingernail grazes the soft skin behind my ear as I try to swat away my anxiety. I really thought that was going to work for a second.

"I don't understand," Laney whines, looking down at her paper. She's not used to not getting her way. If it wasn't such awful timing, I'd be more than amused Laney finally met a magical situation she can't fix.

As it is, though, I'd prefer if she could actually help our strange houseguest.

Luna wipes a few drops of coffee that spilled onto the outside of her mug during her plummet to the floor and then takes another sip. Her eyes meet mine again with a wicked glint in them. I'm not sure why she's so amused by all of this.

"I'm sorry," Laney whimpers. "I tried."

"It's alright, Little—" Luna stops speaking abruptly, as if searching for another word. "It's alright. I trust the two of you to keep my true nature a secret until I'm unbound and free to leave this realm."

"Of course, we wouldn't tell a soul," I rush out. I hate to think she's comparing us to the witches who sacrificed her friend. We aren't those kind of people and if anyone in my family was, I'd fucking riot.

Chapter 7
Unknown

I wave my hand over the water, watching as the minuscule ripples rise and fall in an indiscernible pattern. The scrying pool is nowhere closer to telling me where the Celestial is hiding, but if I say that—

"Have you found it?"

I bite the inside of my cheek at the use of the word 'it'. They aren't 'its', they're extremely powerful beings and if we aren't careful, our coven could be destroyed on our quest to gain immortality.

"I haven't," I admit, dropping the magic connecting me to the water as I step away from the pool. Surrounding me on all sides are a handful of my brothers and sisters. Red robes and black masks make it impossible to tell one from the other, which is sort of the point.

The Order thrives on anonymity.

Chaos thrives on anonymity.

"A Celestial presence has entered our realm," a loud, booming voice echoes around us. I know which hood the voice comes from, but I'm pretty sure I'm one of only a few who does. It's a simple projection spell.

"Why now?" A feminine voice calls out from the fray.

"Do we know which one it is?"

I turn first toward the general direction of the woman, then back toward the man who spoke next. We aren't supposed to know or say each other's names during meetings, but I also know who this idiot is.

Ever since I moved here, this particular coven within The Order has driven me batty.

A growl echoes somewhere in the room, followed by the hiss of an angry cat. I shake my head. "I don't know why, but we must be vigilant. We can't afford to let this opportunity pass us by, not when it's been three thousand years since the last Celestial stepped foot on our world."

"What can we do?"

"We need to figure out where the Celestial is and which one is here, before we make any moves," I offer. I half expect the loud booming voice of our true coven leader to interrupt me, but he doesn't.

"The process of elimination is all we can rely on for now, until the Celestial is located," our leader finally answers. "Blessed be."

"Blessed be," a few dozen voices call back. I watch as body after body retreats from the room, their red hoods pulled low over their faces, even though they're hidden by a mask.

Several familiars prowl along the edge of the room. A large lion, a wolf, and a python narrowly avoid one another as they hug the wall, tracking their witches across the room.

"We can't afford to let this opportunity slip past us," he says directly to me.

"I know that," I scoff. "It's not even a once in a lifetime opportunity, it's a one in thirty lifetimes opportunity. I get it, there's nothin' else I can do until we have more information."

"When you joined our coven, I was promised by your old coven leader that you could add great value to my existing team."

"And I have, for years," I snap, my lips tight as I try to stop speaking. Pissing the coven leader off won't do me any favors, even if I'm right.

"Do not fail me on this. Find the Celestial." With that, the hooded man walks gingerly out of the room, an oversized python slithering along at his heel.

"Fucking prick," I snarl underneath my breath before turning back to the scrying pool. It seems I'll be late picking her up again. She's going to be pissed, but honestly, there's nothing I can do.

"Locus," I murmur as I wave my hand over the calm pool of water once again. Ripples rise and fall and tumble outward toward the edge of the metallic rim.

When I find the Celestial, I won't have to deal with any of this anymore.

Chapter 8
Alandra

I blink owlishly at Luna for what feels like the hundredth time since she started talking this morning. "You want to do what?" I ask again. The woman has lost her mind and there's not enough coffee in the world to fix whatever in the fuck is wrong with her.

"I want to see this Waiting Field you say we are in."

"It's a city, not an actual field, and it's Waitsfield, not Waiting Field." I pinch the bridge of my nose and cross my legs under the table. It's too early to be arguing with another adult, especially one whose supposed to be as old as the Earth itself.

That thought gives me pause as I look across my coffee mug at Luna with fresh eyes. This woman is as old as Earth and look at her. Goddess, I hope I age that well. "No."

"I don't take orders from mortals," Luna sniffs before taking a bite of her bagel. "I'll go with or without you, but it seemed polite to invite you along as my host." She flips her hair over her shoulder with her free hand and I can't help but think she's awfully sassy for an old lady.

"I'm not ordering you, for fucks sake," I groan. "You said you literally felt your friend die because of what he was. And you want to go running around a coven-town because you're curious."

"You brought me here."

"On accident!"

"Still, I'm here. I haven't been to this realm in ages, Alandra. I'm going out after breakfast."

My eyes narrow as I sip my coffee. I haven't had nearly enough caffeine to deal with this level of attitude from anyone other than Beezlebub. I glance around the room, a momentary sense of panic sweeping through me as I search for my beloved monster moth. He sits on the edge of the window sill, perched neatly above a tin of water and fruit slices, seemingly ignoring our argument.

"Whatever."

"What does that mean?" she asks with a grin.

"It means I can't stop you from doing anything you want to do, but this is a pain in my ass and I feel responsible for you. So, whatever."

Luna throws her arms into the air in a victorious way that annoys me to my actual soul. I pick up what's left of my bagel and take a bite, trying to mentally prepare myself for the day ahead.

"What happens to the actual moon while you're stuck here?"

"Nothing. What you see in the sky is just a physical representation of the actual Celestial body." Luna waves her hand down at her own very real body and raises her eyebrows. "As long as I'm in one piece, the lunar cycle will remain unphased."

"Don't you mean it will remain phased?" I snicker at my own joke, deadpanning when Luna's eyebrows crease.

"What?"

"Oh my stars!" I laugh. "The phases of the moon? You know what, it's not important. Forget it." Apparently Earth humor doesn't translate well with Celestials.

Luna stares at me suspiciously and goes back to eating her bagel. "This cream cheese is delicious," she notes.

"Wait until you try the flavored kind."

"There's one with more flavor?" The look of pure shock on her face is so wholesome I can't help the grin pulling at my lips.

"Yeah, hot stuff, there are ones with more flavor. When we go out later, I'll make sure we grab some. You'll love it."

Luna looks away from me but I can still see the pink marring her cheek. Is she blushing?

I yawn against the palm of my hand while we stand in line. Luna fidgets restlessly beside me, drawing my gaze. She'd refused to wear pants when offered, so instead, she's sporting one of the many cotton dresses my mother bought for me that I will never wear and a coat we stealthily borrowed from Laney's closet.

"Why in creation are we standing in this incessant line?" Luna mutters, bumping into my side.

"Because you wanted coffee," I laugh, pointing to the barista doling out paper cups with steam rising from them.

"I didn't realize there would be a wait." She sounds annoyed, but I can't help but be amused. Waiting in line must seem so trivial to her. Behind us, a small girl stands with her mother and begins pointing.

"Mommy, why is her hair white?" At first, I think the child is talking about me. I'm used to people pointing out my odd hair color, I'm much too young to be grey already, but I've had silver and grey in my hair since I was a child. To my surprise though, when I turn around to answer her question, the little girl is pointing at Luna.

"I don't know, baby. Some people have white hair."

I wink at the child and turn back around to find Luna gawking openly at the little girl.

"She's so cute!"

"Thank you," the mother murmurs with a frown as she lays a protective hand on her child's shoulder. I slide my hand through Luna's bent elbow and pull her into my side.

"You can't just gawk at people's kids," I explain. "It makes them uncomfortable."

"What, why? She's adorable and should be told so." Luna begins to turn over her shoulder, probably to address the little girl again, but I stop her.

"No, bad." I cringe as I realize I'm admonishing her like a puppy. "There's a lot of weird stuff in this world and people get protective over their children."

Luna is quiet for a moment before she slides her hand into mine. I squeeze it, acknowledging the way her mouth sags at the corners now. I can't help but feel like I just stole a tiny piece of her joy. There are obviously things in this world she's missed while being in the Celestial realm. The line moves forward and we come one step closer to our goal of delicious, gourmet coffee.

"What kind are you going to get?" I ask, pointing to the large menus above the cashier's head to distract her.

"Hmm," she ponders, laying her free hand across the hollow of her throat. Her stand still rests gingerly in mine, I realize, as I feel a slight tug on my wrist.

Glancing down at my hand, a warmth spreads in my chest. It's probably just her way, she's completely out of my league. Hell, we don't even live in the same plane of existence. But this is the first time I've gone a whole day without thinking about Jess. Well, until now. My head rocks back and forth as I let that thought tumble through my brain like a cartwheel. I haven't thought about Jess at all, really, since Luna showed up.

Accidentally endangering the most commonly called upon Celestial in the witching community could distract anyone. You're probably not over it yet, so stop obsessing. I roll my eyes at the voice in the back of my head. As critical as my parents are, no one is as critical of me as me. I can be a real bitch, sometimes.

"The tuxedo mocha sounds good," Luna finally answers. "White chocolate and milk chocolate and coffee mixed together. I think I want that." Her bright eyes meet mine and I smile at her, squeezing her hand.

Her gaze drops to our joined fingers and she quickly pulls out of my hold, a blush creeping across her cheeks. "Apologies," she murmurs.

I shrug, blowing out a heavy sigh as I turn back toward the line that inches forward in front of us. My phone vibrates in my pocket and I pull it free, wincing at the string of emojis from Laney.

"Mad face, mad face, knife emoji, question mark, question mark, exclamation point." I blink down at my phone, watching the three little dots dance in a line as Laney types her next message.

LANEY: WHERE THE FUCK ARE YOU GUYS?

"Ohhh, she is *not* happy that we went out." I slip the phone back into my pocket, deciding to ignore the next few vibrations. I don't feel like being lectured and Luna hasn't even gotten her penguin latte or whatever it was she was going to get.

"Does she always insert herself in your private affairs?"

"Yes," I answer, without hesitation. "Always. Laney is what we call a prodigy, I'm not sure if there was a different word for it the last time you were around witches—"

"I'm familiar with the concept."

"I'm not."

"No, you're not," Luna agrees, smiling at me with kind eyes. "But there is something inside you which isn't inside Laney. She has a lot of magic at her disposal, just under her skin where she can access it without trying. You have a potential of a different sort. The ability to hone your skill is a completely different conversation, and not one I want to have today, but you're gifted in your own way, Alandra."

My head catches to the side as I look at her. She looks completely serious. There's no power hiding inside me. I'm completely and utterly ordinary, as everyone in my life had been pointing out for the past twenty-nine years. There's nothing special about me at all except for the fact that I have absolutely no talent in a family full of prodigies. Still, her words sound so close to ones my Grandma used to tell me that my heart aches.

"Stop doubting my words, Little Witch," Luna hisses as she takes a step up to the counter. "I'll have a tuxedo mocha, please," she tells the cashier in a kind voice.

Behind us, a tiny giggle sounds off followed by a quiet, "Shhh."

I glance over my shoulder in time to catch the little girl Luna had been so infatuated with pointing at her long white hair.

"Mommy, she's so pretty," she murmurs in awe.

"Shh, darling. We don't talk to strangers." I nod politely and turn back around to tell the cashier my order, but Luna is waiting with two cups in hand. My eyebrows shoot up my forehead as I take one of the cups from her.

"We shall see how good this tuxedo is together." She presses the cup to her lips and takes a small sip, her eyes falling shut as we walk away from the counter. "Oh my Goddess," she moans.

My throat tightens as the sound drifts between us like a soft melody played at night when no one's around. Her voice reminds me of the kind of music you make love to. Her voice reminds me of making love.

"That good, huh?" I laugh, trying to cover my inappropriate thoughts.

"It's divine!" She bobs her head quickly, her eyes sparkling with delight as she waits for me to try mine.

I grimace at the cup and take a slow sip, careful not to burn my tongue. "Oh my Goddess, you're right," I sputter. I'd never tasted anything like it before. Did she spell the damned coffee? "This is the tuxedo penguin thing you ordered?"

"Tuxedo mocha," she corrects me. "It's the absolute best beverage I've had in *any* realm."

"I have to remember the name of it," I agree as we walk toward the parking lot. "Wait. How did you pay for this?"

"Pay?" Luna asks with a frown.

"Oh Goddess," I mumble, glancing back at the long line of patrons waiting for their warm treats. I'm tempted to run back and pay for it, but I do enough business at the shop, I'll pay for it the next time I come around.

The ground is slick with ice and small mountains of plowed snow decorate the lot at each side and corner. We fall into a comfortable silence as make our way to my car. It's not awkward, but definitely full of things that I want to say.

"What made you say all of that back there?" I ask as I open the driver door, looking at Luna over the top of the car.

"Because it's true, Little Witch. You doubt me?"

"Yes," I admit carefully. "But only because I know I don't have some secret affinity hiding anywhere inside me. Trust me, my family would have dragged it out of me by now." I duck into the car and quickly crank it as Luna gets herself situated. Heat blasts from the vents and my eyes roll shut as the warmth starts to filter through the chilly car.

"You shouldn't, and like I said, it's not an affinity." Luna curls her feet underneath herself, completely ignoring the seat belt which should be buckled. I bite my tongue, far be it from me to parent an immortal. Can she even die from something physical like that?

"I'd feel safer if you had your seatbelt on," I finally admit as I pull the car into traffic. The small town of Waitsfield has always been a little bit busier than normal this time of year. During Yule, even humans will travel to coven-towns like ours for blessed candles and small amounts of spellwork for their holiday.

Some of them don't really believe in the magic they're given, and admittedly, some of them end up getting ripped off. There was a news piece done a few years ago that detailed how it was illegal to sell something under the guise of being magical/spelled if it wasn't. Nothing ever came of it, though. I mean, how exactly are human law enforcement agencies supposed to enforce laws on magical products? How would they be able to prove anything in their courts?

"This thing?" She pulls the belt across her chest with a hard yank, snarling when the mechanism catches and she can't pull it any farther.

"Uh, yeah, that's the one." I reach over, pulling slowly on the belt until it stretches out to an acceptable length. "Move slower so it doesn't catch. It goes in the little buckle to your left." With my eyes back on the road, I try not to laugh at all the squirming going on out of the corner of my eye. "Do you got it?"

"I think so." A soft click tells me the buckle is secure and I look to my right to find Luna turned around in her seat, her back to the windshield, staring at the newly buckled seat belt. "I don't understand how this helps at all—"

"Oh my Goddess," I laugh. "Get back in your seat before you get me a ticket."

"What in creation is a ticket? For what?"

I bite my lip, trying not to laugh. She's just too damn cute. How could someone be so damn powerful but so fucking clueless at the same time?

"Just put your back against the seat and sit still, please."

"Fine." She turns around and crosses her arms over her chest, staring out the window. Chuckling quietly to myself, I switch on the radio.

"And today on WTCHXM we have Madison in Connecticut."

"Hi, River, thank you. I just wanted to say I think it's crazy how many

coven-towns still allow animal sacrifice under their covenant. It's a disgrace. This isn't the dark ages! There's other ways for witches to fuel their magic—"

"Well, sacrifice has been around for quite some time, Madison."

"So has murder."

"Alrighty then, why don't we—"

A pale hand fumbles across the dash. When the station changes and the speakers blast a song with rhythmic bass, Luna scrambles across the display again, her hand finally landing on the right knob. She manages to turn the volume almost all the way down and I glance at her face out of the corner of my eye.

"What's wrong?"

"I don't want to hear them argue the necessity of sacrifice. It's not necessary, if you're wondering. Not usually."

I want to ask what she means or when it *is* necessary, but it's painfully obvious she doesn't want to talk about it so I change the subject. "Laney is going to try to send you home again, I bet."

"It's a waste of time," Luna sighs. "I'm here for the time being. I've decided to look at it as a . . . break. I may as well enjoy the time I have in this realm. When I get home, I'll have to strengthen my wards. The fact that a witch was able to summon me here against my will means they must be growing weak."

"Mm," I hum quietly, drumming my fingers on the steering wheel as we turn onto my street. "Do you ever get lonely?"

"Well—" Luna clears her throat, and the rustle of fabric beside me tells me she's fidgeting with her dress again. "Yes, I suppose I do."

As the car inches up the driveway, I turn and look at Luna fully. My question is beyond inappropriate, but when else would I get a chance to ask?

"Do Celestials, you know—" I wave my hand vaguely before putting the car in park. "Copulate?"

"What now?"

"You know. Do you, umm, make babies?" My cheeks grow hot as Luna stares blankly at me from the passenger seat. She blinks, then a boisterous laugh fills the car.

"Heavens no. I couldn't imagine!"

"Well, then what?" I shrug nonchalantly and pull the keys from the ignition, then grab the coffee cup with my name sprawled across it. It's spelled wrong, of course, but the poor barista did his best. *Elandrea.* I shudder. Okay, maybe that's not his best.

"You want to know if we have lovers?" Luna smooths her hair down against the side of her face and nods slowly. "Yes. Sometimes other Celestials, sometimes humans or witches, historically. But since we closed our realms," she sighs. "It's really just us and we all stay so separated."

"That does sound lonely." I shake my head as I push the car door open and contemplate the cold jog to the front door. Undoubtedly, Laney is in there, waiting to ambush poor Luna with some half-cooked plan to get her back to her realm. She isn't used to her magic being ineffective. Hell, she isn't used to not getting her way at all.

"It's a different sort of existence," she admits, stroking a lock of hair repeatedly.

"It's strange to imagine the Celestials bumping uglies," I laugh. "So you're dating the sun, right?" Her eyes go round, like they might pop right out of her head as she shakes her head.

"Absolutely not! He's incorrigible. Personally, I view the other Celestials as a sort of family. Romanticizing them would be hard for me."

"Ah," I hum, nodding my own head. "That makes sense." My lips part with another question but the front door to the house swings open, cutting off my train of thought.

Laney stands at the door, waving her hand as if beckoning us inside. I groan. Luna laughs. My head shakes from side to side as I grab Luna's coffee cup from the cup holder and shut the door. A rogue snowflake lands on the tip of my nose and I scrunch it around trying to get it off.

Luna catches up to me quickly, flicking the little thing off of me before she makes her way inside. I can't help but smile as I follow her through the door. Laney grabs my elbow before I get two feet inside and I stop, staring down at her.

"What's up?"

"Don't get attached to her, Bug," she whispers. Her eyes look softer than normal, like she's emotional. My eyebrows draw down low and I shake my head.

"I don't know what you're—"

"That's cool," she interrupts, standing on her tiptoes to peer around my shoulder after Luna. "Just don't do it. She'll be gone soon and I don't want to see you broken again like you were with Jess."

I swallow and nod, then turn around and head into the living room where Luna sits, draped across the couch like she belongs there.

Maybe she's right. Maybe I need to be more careful.

Luna grabs the cup of coffee from my hand and smiles up at me, her lips curving in a delicious display.

Yep. Being careful, starting now.

"HAVE YOU HEARD FROM MOM?" LANEY ASKS BETWEEN SIPS OF TEA. HER short hair is a mess, displaced from her fingers running through it in frustration. It turns out she'd brought home several old books about Celestials and Celestial magic to try and send Luna home. We'd read chapter after chapter, skimmed spell after spell, and still hadn't found a single thing that could help us.

"I haven't, why?" I close the book closest to me and yawn. It's getting late, Luna already excused herself to go take a shower. I keep telling Laney there's nothing in here that can help us, but she seems determined to 'beat' this spell.

"She texted me. Something about Dad working extra hours and she's worried about him."

"Oh," I mutter. *That's not good.* "You don't think he's having another aff—"

"Don't even say it," Laney groans. "I really fucking hope not. I checked out his social media and everything looks good." Beezlebub lands on her shoulder, probably because she's getting anxious—he's always been sensitive to people's emotions—and Laney shoos him away. "Ew, B, no!" she hisses, visibly shuddering.

Beezlebub chitters as he makes his way, lazily, toward me. He lands on my shoulder and I run a finger down his furry torso. *Poor B, he was just trying to help.*

Dad loves Mom, that much I know, but he has been known to have a wandering eye. And that wandering eye of his has been known to get him into trouble on occasion. The last time, we were still in high school. Laney and I came home from school and found Mom crying over a cup of tea, shaking her head as if she was disagreeing with someone talking to her.

The thing about living with a medium, is lying to them is nearly impossible. If they're good at what they do, the spirits will rat your ass out before anyone else can. It's tiresome. Dad should know better by now.

"I hope everything's okay. We should check on her."

"Well, dinner is in what, two days?" Laney glances down at her phone, checking her calendar, I guess. "Yeah. We will make sure to remind her how awesome she is."

"And how much of an idiot he is."

"Yeah, that too."

I shake my head and stand up, yawning against my hand. "Goodnight, Firefly."

"Goodnight, Bug."

As I make my way toward the hallway, I trip on something large and soft. The strangest squeak possible comes out of my mouth as I go flying toward the ground. Luckily, the thing I tripped on is Juniper. I land on a soft pile of furry spots just as a yowl claws its way out of her throat.

"Sorry, girl." I scratch the fur behind her ears and scurry to my feet, making my way to my bedroom before I can cause anymore scenes. It's been a long day. Between showing Luna around Waitsfield and being forced to research magic with Laney, I'm exhausted.

I throw myself face down onto my bed with a satisfied grunt and just lay there. Existing. Today is finally over. The sound of water running in the bathroom lulls me into a relaxed, not-quite-asleep, almost meditative state. Rolling onto my side, my eyes slide shut as the dark room envelopes me. It's cozy in here, warmer than it should be, but I'm not complaining.

I don't know how I long I lay there, soaking up the quiet darkness, before the bathroom door cracks open and light filters through into my peaceful oasis. The light fades away and I open my eyes and take in a view I probably shouldn't, but I can't tear my eyes away.

Luna stands with her back to me, long wet hair trailing down her spine as she rifles through the pile of dresses on my dresser I'd set aside for her. I'm never going to wear them, so she might as well enjoy them while she's here. I swallow, trying to ignore the way my core clenches when she bends at the waist to open a drawer—the one I keep my socks in. The soft curve of her hips gives way to a beautiful, round ass, the kind you'd have to spend months on squats to get. *I wonder if Celestials have to exercise.*

When she's done pulling the socks onto her feet, she stands upright again and begins pulling a dress over her head. She turns around, the dress not quite past her face yet and I nearly groan.

I thought her breasts were beautiful in the see-through excuse of a dress she'd shown up here wearing. I had no idea what I was talking about. Pink, pebbled nipples stand at attention on her soft, creamy tits. The dress falls down her body and my eyes rocket up to her face.

Shit.

"You're awake," she notes, walking toward the bed.

"Mhm." My cheeks burn with embarrassment. She has to know I was checking her out. I slide my arm under my pillow and lay my head back down, focusing on anything other than the slick need building between my thighs.

"The mortal realm has changed *a lot* since I last visited." Luna sits down onto the bed beside me and fans her hair out on the pillow above her head, her chin tilted slightly in my direction..

"I'd imagine so. Civilizations have risen and fallen since you were last here. A few times. It's got to be weird for you."

"It is. I remember coming to Earth often, for Moon rituals. Fertility magic was one of my favorites to witness, but now, I only get to hear the songs and spells from a distance."

"That's really sad," I whisper, chewing my lip.

"It is." She turns her face toward me fully now. Her eyes meet mine and my breath hitches for a moment. Her skin has this habit of glowing in the dark, but then again, so does the moon. It makes sense. Her eyes remind me of the night sky, right now. Gone is the light silver hue I'd quickly grown accustomed to, replaced by a not quite blue, but definitely not black either.

Luna reaches a hand out, hesitantly, and cups my cheek before she pulls away a lock of my silvery blonde hair. "This hair reminds me of home," she purrs. "It's like looking into a distorted mirror." She drops the hair and slides her hand smoothly across my cheek, behind my ear. Her nails against my scalp send goosebumps down my neck and across my skin. My eyes widen as she leans closer, a half-dry lock of hair falling down the side of her face. She stops, less than an inch from my mouth, her lips parted, and searches my eyes for something.

"Yes," I whisper, sliding my hand around her throat to the nape of her neck. It's a terrible idea. It has to be the worst fucking idea I've ever had but I don't care. Right now, with her in my bed, her skin glowing softly in the darkness, her rosy lips parted for me . . . I can't tell her no.

She presses her lips to mine gently, plucking at them with her own. Our mouths move together like water, teasing, testing. When my tongue slides across her bottom lip, she shivers in my arms and a jolt of pure lust shoots through me. Luna's leg slides over my hip and my hand falls to her thigh, holding her against me as my tongue slips between the seam of her lips.

"We should stop," she moans breathily into my mouth as my tongue slides over hers. A shudder courses through my body as her hips grind once, twice, three times against my thigh. Slowly, Luna pulls back from the kiss, a little breathless.

"Goodnight, Alandra Michaels," she whispers, her chest rising and falling quickly.

"Goodnight, Luna," I murmur, smoothing her hair back away from her face. She smiles at me before rolling over and pulling my hand around her waist. I kiss the back of her shoulder, trying to keep my breath even as I listen to her fall asleep.

Don't get attached. Laney's voice rings in my ears and I roll my eyes heavenward. Something in me knows this is going to be brutal. But something else in me knows I'm powerless to stop it.

Chapter 9
Luna

Everything blurs around me for a moment and I shiver as the presence of someone else's consciousness washes over me. Alandra is here in this dreamscape somewhere.

Dragging my fingers across the seam between my consciousness and Alandra's, I press until a faint shimmer spreads throughout the air around me. As her mental walls come down, Alandra's dreamscape becomes clearer. I can feel her somewhere close, but in distress.

I close my eyes, reaching out for her with my mind, and when I open them again, Alandra is standing before me. Against the backdrop of an empty, grey room, Alandra shakes her head as another woman speaks.

"I'm taking the job in California," this mysterious woman whispers. I narrow my eyes on her, my arms crossing my chest as I try to figure out who my Little Witch is dreaming of. She's a pretty thing—shorter than me, shorter even than Alandra. Her hair is painted a muted pink and pastel blue. While she's not my personal preference, her thin frame suits the angles of her face.

"Why would you do this to me?" Alandra's voice is barely a whimper. Her shoulders heave with pent up emotion. It's easy to see she's doing her best not to cry, to be reasonable.

"Because I don't love you." The girl turns around, giving her back to Alandra. Whatever control my Little Witch had over her emotions snaps like a cord drawn too tight. Her shoulders shake with the tears coursing down her face.

"None of us love you," a male voice interjects. My eyes scan the man as he enters the scene. He has light colored hair and blazing blue eyes. The resemblance between the two is uncanny. This has to be her father.

"You're nothing but a burden."

"You've never been good enough." The disembodied voices echo off the walls. Laney's voice stands out above the rest. What would make Alandra torture herself this way? Does she really believe all this nonsense?

Once I decide I've seen enough of this self-inflicted torture, I wave my hand and the scene changes. Alandra looks around at the new environment. No more colorless walls. No more angry lovers or emotionally abusive family members. Now, she is surrounded by a peaceful field of moon blossoms.

"That's better," I murmur.

Her head snaps to the side as if she's chasing the sound of my voice and I grin to myself, calling out a little louder this time. "Your worth isn't determined by those around you."

"I've never been enough for them," she sighs, dropping to her knees in the middle of the tall lavender grass amidst the silver flowers.

Walking toward her, I hold out my hand. Her fingertips brush mine and then I'm in her arms. I didn't make that change. Alandra actually wants this? Her lips crash onto mine with a hurried need, pulling my hips against hers. I blink, hesitating for only a second before I return the kiss with just as much need. It's been so long. . .

My fingers bunch in the back of her shirt as colors fade around us. I get lost inside the heat of her mouth until there's nothing in this universe we created but us two. My back hits something soft as Alandra moves on top of me, straddling my hips. She bends down, swiping her lips against mine.

My chest rises as falls as I chase her lips, her hands sliding over my body. Her anxiety still takes up space in the dreamscape, causing the abstract colors her mind summoned to swirl around us like an angry storm.

With the flick of a hand, the scene changes and Alandra is on her back. Her eyes widen as I crawl up her body. My fingers run across the fabric of her pants and they dissolve under my touch. Pushing her shirt slowly up her stomach and over her breasts, I hold her gaze as that restrictive piece of fabric disappears, too. She's naked beneath me, her skin trembling beneath my touch. I lower my head down to her breast, whispering against the flesh as my tongue darts out to tease her nipple. "Let me take care of you."

My mouth closes around the pink nub and her hand flies into my hair, holding me against her while I suck and my tongue swirls.

"Yes," she murmurs fervently. Her back arches, pushing both of us up a little and I roll my hips against hers to ground us. My hand snakes between us, massaging her hip and thigh as I kiss across her breast to her collar bone. My teeth trace gently over the skin before I move up, kissing along her neck to her ear.

"Tell me, Little Witch, how badly you want me," I moan against her ear, my tongue tracing over the sensitive skin there as I speak to her. "Tell me what you need."

Alandra chokes out a strangled whimper, her fingers digging into my lower back, pulling me closer. Her dreamscape makes our movements seem fluid, even to me. My thigh rubs against her seam and she shudders, rolling her hips, chasing that delicious friction we both crave.

"I want you," she whispers. The light around us changes but I refuse to look away from her as I move down her body. My tongue traces a swirling line from the top of her breast down her belly until I find the top of her pussy. Raking my nails down her sides, I sigh against the outside of her folds. My tongue slips through and traces its way up to her clit.

"Th-that," she mumbles as her fingers wind through my hair. The pressure on my scalp urges me on, my tongue twirling around her clit. Her hips buck against my mouth and I grin to myself.

"So needy," I purr, sliding my hand down her thigh. The tip of my finger circles her opening, testing how wet she is before I slide inside. When I pull my finger back I slide another in with it, curling them against the precious spot tucked just inside her.

"Fuck! Luna!" Her voice breaks when I latch onto her clit, sucking the sensitive nub while my fingers pump in and out of her, over and over. My tongue lashes out against her clit, my free hand holding her hips to my face as she arches her back.

"Please," she whimpers. My tongue slows and I raise up, looking down at her face as my fingers massage her g-spot, the flat of my hand bumping against her clit with every movement.

"Please what?"

"Please! Please let me cum, Goddess, please," she moans, her eyes locked on to mine. A shudder curves my spine and I bend down, pressing my mouth

to hers, adding a third finger. The pressure must be too much, because she trembles beneath me, her eyes squeezing shut as her pussy spasms against my hand.

"That's it," I murmur, coaxing every last wave of pleasure I can from her body before the dreamscape fades away.

"Goddess, what I wouldn't give for this to be real," she whispers as the thin veil breaks and light begins to shine into my waking eyes.

Chapter 10
Alandra

Staring at myself in the bathroom mirror, I let my hands fill with some cool water and quickly splash it against my cheeks. I'd woken up in a frenzy. That dream was . . . intense, to say the very fucking least.

"Are you almost done?" Luna asks from the bedroom. I quickly rush to the door and make sure the tiny lock is turned so she can't come in. I can't face her right now. Part of me knows it's just a product of sharing a bed with someone for the first time in a while, but another—and much bigger—part of me is mortified I'd had such a steamy dream about Luna.

What the fuck is wrong with you? I ask myself accusingly as I glare at the mirror. My cheeks are still pink. Hell, I can still feel her mouth on me if I close my eyes. I shake my head and brace myself on the sink. I absolutely am not going to obsess over this. It's just a proximity thing, I'm sure. And the fact that she's basically a Goddess has to play a factor. I'm sure she's alluring to everyone. *I'm not alone in my little perversion, right?*

With a growl, I force a brush through my mussed hair and focus on calm, socially appropriate thoughts. If I play it cool, everything will be fine. That's the mantra I repeat to myself as I open the bathroom door and come face to face with the seductress herself.

"Are you alright?" she asks, her mouth swishing to the side as she meets my eyes.

"Yeah, I'm fine. Bathroom's all free," I mumble as I slide past her.

Luna turns the slightest bit to watch me move past her and the small movement causes my arm to brush against hers. My cheeks flame red. I can't see them, but I sure can feel the heat they're throwing off, it's like a damn sunburn.

"Oh! Sorry!" I force a polite smile on my face as Luna steadies me with a hand on my arm. She eyes me suspiciously for a moment but then releases me and heads into the bathroom, closing the door behind her. I take the few steps necessary to reach the bed and face-plant into it, groaning into the soft comforter.

"Whyyyy?"

"What was that?" Luna calls with a muffled voice from the bathroom.

"Nothing!" My heart thunders against my ribcage as I try to think of a lie. "Just going to grab some food." I shake my head slowly as I realize how idiotic I sound. This is ridiculous.

It's not like I'm some fucking virgin, what the hell is wrong with me?

I pull myself together enough to at least stand up from the bed and grab my hoodie. Nothing like a comfort item to keep you grounded, right? As I pull it over my head, the familiar scent and feeling of safety washes over me and I make my way toward the door with more confidence.

This is going to be fine.

But all I can picture is the meme with the dog in a burning café.

I STRIDE INTO THE LIVING ROOM, FEELING MUCH LESS SELF-CONSCIOUS than I did a few minutes ago. Beezlebub lands on my shoulder and I run a finger down his wings absentmindedly as he chitters away at me.

"Good morning to you, too," I mumble to him between a yawn.

"You good?" Laney asks from the kitchen table, her hands securely wrapped around a mug of tea. My eyes drift from her to the extra decorations in the room. There's more red in here than there was yesterday, more greenery too.

"Did you decorate more?"

"Yeah, Marcus is supposed to come over later. He feels bad we didn't bring you to his Yule party." Laney beams at me over the mug before taking another sip and I shudder at the thought of having to deal with her weird boyfriend.

"Laney, about Marcus—"

"He's amazing, right?" She sounds so damned happy and my heart sinks with guilt. It's like a stone in my stomach, uncomfortable and heavy. With the blessing and then Luna showing up, I haven't managed to tell her what a creep her *amazing* boyfriend is.

"He's . . . something," I manage. Maybe I was imagining the creepiness with Marcus. Even as the thought crosses my mind, I know in my heart, it isn't true. That guy is a snake. As I tiptoe around Juniper and make my way into the kitchen for some kind of food, the sound of a door popping open catches my ear. My heart races again and I groan, mentally cursing my awkwardness.

Why are you like this?

Had it been this weird when I met Jess? Admittedly, I don't date a lot. Jess was the first real girlfriend I've had. I tried dating guys before that, mainly because the only gay girls in Waitsfield are mega-goths. Not that there's anything wrong with that, I've just never really found black lipstick that appealing. I shudder a little as I open the refrigerator, my silent musings keeping me at least somewhat occupied as Luna comes into the room. Even I can feel the power radiating off of her when she comes in. She takes up a lot of space for someone so small.

"Oh, I love Yule," Luna coos from the living room.

"I'm glad you approve of the decorations," Laney laughs. "It's still sort of bizarre."

"Only a little," I mutter, turning around with a few cubes of cheese in my hand. As I eat them, Luna comes to sit at the table with Laney, whose already pouring her some tea.

"Well, it won't last forever," Luna replies, looking up to me with a sad smile. No, it won't last forever, and maybe that's part of why I'm freaking out.

Luna's presence in my home should have been way more disrupting than it has. Instead, she's come in here and assimilated into our household in the past few days like she's always been there. In a way, I suppose she has. I've always been drawn to moon magic above anything else. I've also always been one to sit under the moon and pout and whine about all my problems. I suddenly wonder if she hears those conversations in the Celestial realm and a new pang of anxiety worms its way through my chest.

"That's true," Laney murmurs, her gaze slowly drifting in my direction. I can feel the implication of her stare boring into my very being. I've known my sister long enough to know when she's judging me. Laney knows she was right and I can't stand the pitiful look in her eyes.

"Who is coming over?" Luna asks, pulling me back to reality.

"Her boyfriend." I roll my eyes and pop another cube of cheese into my mouth as the girls dissolve into a strangely normal conversation about boyfriends, Yule, and how the various decorations around the house help balance out the flow of energy this time of year.

I shake my head and turn to grab a tea bag. Maybe there's some water left in the kettle.

I WALK TO THE DOOR WITH A GROAN, IGNORING THE SECOND—AND much more annoying—ring of the doorbell with every ounce of self-control I can muster. As I pull the door open, I realize our houseguest has no intention of waiting for me to invite him in. He's already pushing past me.

"Welcome," I growl under my breath.

"Blessed Yule!" Marcus tosses me a wink over his shoulder before he moves on to greeting everyone else in the house. "My love!" he murmurs to Laney and a cold shiver runs down my spine. That guy is slimier than a snail.

"Marcus," Laney laughs, pawing at his hands as they come around her in an embarrassingly intimate hug. "We have a guest."

He clears his throat and looks from the kitchen to the living room where Luna sits watching TV. "Oh, my," he laughs. "I'm so rude, forgive me. I'm Marcus, it's very nice to meet you—"

"Luna," I supply as I walk toward them.

"Our . . ." Laney looks to me frantically, her eyes going wide as she tries to think of a lie. My head shakes to the side but I'm too late, she's already trying to force the lie out. "Cousin."

"Your cousin? I didn't think you had any." His tone isn't accusatory, just interested. My hands clench at my sides as I watch his eyes drift over Luna's body. He still has an arm around my sister's waist and is leering at another woman!

"Turns out we do!" I grind my teeth, trying to stop talking. There's no telling what will come out of my mouth if I get started.

"I'm very pleased to make your acquaintance, Marcus," Luna calls from the couch. "And a very blessed Yule to you."

He grins at me as if he's won something and I roll my eyes. The man is disgusting. I don't understand how my sister doesn't see him for the snake he is, but she's already moved into the kitchen to finish preparing our meal.

Marcus leans against the wall, straddling the invisible line which separates the kitchen from the living room. I shake my head and ignore him as Laney stirs something on the stove. I'm not even sure what she made.

Luna sits on the back of the couch, her feet on the cushions she *should* be sitting on, watching TV with child-like enthusiasm. "This movie is spectacular!"

"That's an Old Spice commercial," I snort. With a shake of my head I make my way into the living room. Marcus's gaze burns a hole in the back of my head—or ass—as I cross the room. I'm even more annoyed with him than I thought I'd be, because in addition to being a creep around me, he seems to be into Luna as well.

"Let the girl enjoy her commercial." His deep voice drips with all the sweetness of honey and my stomach rolls. Ignoring him is hard, but I manage to do it, even as he begins whispering to Laney.

"Who is she really?"

"She's our cousin." Laney sounds uncomfortable but I refuse to look back. It'll only prove to him that we're lying. *Goddess, how I wish she hadn't tried to lie. She's never been good at it.*

"You're a terrible liar, love," he murmurs in the same tone he'd used a moment ago when speaking to me. Rage boils deep in my stomach but I focus on Luna.

Her head turns to the side, her eyes meeting mine as I lean against the back of the couch. Without saying a word, Luna raises a hand and lays it on my back, rubbing it in small circles. The warmth in her touch sends butterflies shooting through my stomach.

"It'll be alright," she whispers softly.

"What?"

"I don't know, but I know his spirit troubles yours." Her voice is less than a whisper. It's a breath of air I can barely hear drifting between us.

My head bobs as her words sink in. "It does." My shoulder bumps against hers as I lean closer, trying to keep our conversation private. "How do you know it will be alright?"

"I don't think he's as bad as he seems. His heart seems pure, even if his mind clouds his judgment."

I glance over my shoulder at the smooth operator currently wrapping his arms around my sister and shake my head. I wish I could see what she sees, but all I see is darkness.

"Stop doubting me," Luna laughs, shoving my shoulder.

My fingers slip off the back of the couch and I stumble, a grin splitting my face. She's right, of course. Who am I to argue with the Moon? I hop over the back of the couch, plopping down into the well worn cushions as the reality show comes back on. It's a new twist on an old classic, Sabrina the Teenage Witch, except in this version, Sabrina is actually a witch. The girl in question was adopted by humans and on her thirteenth birthday, when her powers manifested, all kinds of questions came up.

The show follows her everyday life and her search for her parents. I wonder, sometimes, what could drive a witch to give her daughter up for adoption. We're a very sex positive community, for the most part. We have an understanding of sexuality that humans take decades to reach, if they ever reach it.

"This is interesting," Luna murmurs from behind me. She's still perched on the back of the couch, her legs dangling to my left. Elbowing her calf lightly, I laugh.

"Shh and watch it."

I'm not sure how long we sit like that before the oven timer goes off. I hop up from couch on instinct and accidentally startle Luna, sending her tumbling down from her strange seat. Luckily, she manages to fall against my chest when I turn around and I throw my arms around her. Her chin bumps into my shoulder, followed by a loud clack of teeth.

We stand like that for a second, her face buried in my shoulder and my arms snug around her back before we finally step apart. Luna's cheeks flame under my attention and I grin. At least I'm not the only self-conscious person in the house anymore. Though, I have no idea why she'd be embarrassed. It was technically my fault, after all.

"Sorry," I rush out, realizing I still hadn't apologized.

"It's alright." Luna runs a hand down the side of my face before she turns toward the kitchen. As my gaze follows her, I see Marcus watching with a smirk.

"Cousins, huh?" He shrugs and makes his way to the counter to grab a plate. He smacks Laney's ass with the dish and my eyes threaten to roll so far back into my head, they can see brain matter.

Luna chuckles quietly, her shaking shoulders the only thing that gives away her amusement. *Oh great, now she thinks he's funny.* Taking a deep, calming breath, I take my seat at the table. Luna hovers awkwardly near the edge of the table before finally taking a seat to my left. In the circular seating, it puts her between Laney and myself, and the farthest from Marcus. I quickly say a little prayer of thanks for that small win.

"So, *Luna*, where are you from?" Marcus asks as he meticulously slices through his chicken. Panic seizes my chest as my eyes meet Laney's across the table.

"Iceland," I quickly interject just as Luna begins to open her mouth. She arches an eyebrow and then nods her head in agreement.

"Ah-huh," Marcus hums. "And what's that like? I've always wanted to go to Reykjavík."

"Travel is so important," Luna answers diplomatically as she stabs a piece of squash on her plate.

"What part are you from? How long are you in town for?"

My eyes bore into Marcus, narrowing as I prepare to tell him exactly what I think about all his nosey ass questions.

"Baby," Laney laughs, waving her fork in accusation. "Stop grilling her."

Marcus holds his hands up in mock surrender, a sly smile on his face. "My apologies! I've just never met an Icelandic Witch before. You feel very powerful, Luna. Even more powerful than my Laney."

"And that's what's important to you, isn't it?" I ask before I can stop myself. "Power."

"Bug!" Laney snaps. Marcus' eyes bore into mine as he mulls over my words. "Stop it, right now, you two."

"Power is one of those things that can only make a partner more attractive, Alandra," he finally laughs, waving away the tension between us. "Like money or good looks."

"How true," Luna replies dryly. "What do you have to offer my . . . cousin?" She glances to me for a moment, as if confirming that's the proper cover story. Luna's arms cross over her chest, her head leaned back against the chair in defiance as she calls the asshole out.

Laney laughs.

Marcus lets out a little shocked gasp.

I don't think she's ever been hotter than she is right now. The confidence combined with that cute little 'That's the right word, right?' look does something strange to my insides.

Marcus recovers quickly and begins twirling his finger in a slow circle. Soon, the salt and pepper shaker begin to spiral around one another through the air, as if dancing. My eyes track the flying objects across the room until they finally return to their spot in the middle of the table.

"How quaint." Luna sounds less than impressed and I can't help but laugh. Laney bites her lip against her own laughter even as Marcus' face flames.

"Well, what about you then? Maybe you're not as powerful as you feel."

Luna smiles, holding Marcus' gaze. All at once every cabinet in the kitchen opens. The microwave door pops free and the oven door crashes to the floor. The sound of the living room door blowing open echoes through the house as well. Several thumps resound around us. I know that sound, that's the sound of a door handle bouncing off a wall.

The quick scraping of windows raising forces me to cringe and shut my eyes momentarily. I've always been sensitive to sound.

The lights flicker as the TV channel changes over and over and the old stereo I can't convince myself to get rid of begins blaring music.

"Alright, we get it," Marcus grinds out.

Luna clasps her hands primly in front of her face and grins at the asshole. An overwhelming sense of pride and amusement sweeps through me as I watch Marcus grow increasingly uncomfortable.

"Well, that sure showed *her*," I laugh at him, scooting away from the table. This amount of fuckery requires wine. Lots of wine. I grab the bottle of red from the counter and pull four glasses down from the rack above the sink.

Laney tries her hardest to coax Marcus into a better mood by promising to do 'that thing he likes'. Shuddering as I try desperately to push those mental images out of my mind, I turn back toward the table. I'm always playing waiter at these things, for some reason. I stop at Luna first, and fill her glass until she begins fingering the rim. Watching her fingertip circle the edge of the glass is hypnotic and I find it hard to look away until she stops moving.

My eyes raise to hers and she smiles at me. *Fucking hell.* I set my glass in front of my chair and pour until it's a little overfull, but like I said, this much fuckery requires wine.

Next I move to Laney, whose glass I only fill half as full. She has a habit of overdoing it, after all.

"Really?" she asks with a roll of her eyes.

I just shrug and move past Marcus, setting his glass and the bottle down as I make my way around to my own seat again. Before I drink the beautiful lifeblood of the Gods, the nectar of everything wonderful, the red wine of my dreams . . . I take a quick sniff. No, I have no clue *why* I sniff the wine. I saw it done in a movie when I was a child and I've done it ever since. It makes me feel fancy, like dressing up in a tutu and fairy wings on your birthday.

Not that I've done that. Recently.

"So what do you girls have planned for the rest of Yule? Anything special for the solstice?" Marcus pours the wine until his glass is half full and does the same thing as me. When he sniffs his wine, he looks like an absolute douche and I suddenly wonder if that's how I seem.

Well, fuck.

"We have dinner with my parents, but the solstice will probably be pretty chill around here."

"Bullshit. Come to my place. We're having a huge party to celebrate," Marcus purrs. "You two are welcome as well, of course."

"I think I'm good," I mutter before taking a long swallow of wine.

Luna just laughs and sips at her wine before standing. "I'm sure it will be a lovely party. I, however, don't socialize with witches who believe themselves to be more than they are."

All of us stare openly at her for a moment in shock. Laney looks like she can't decide between screaming or laughing. Marcus' cheeks turn bright red and I nearly spit my wine out.

With that, Luna slips her fingers through her long hair and walks from the room. I could swear her hips sway a little more than necessary as she makes her exit.

Laney is the first to break the silence at the table. "What the fuck was that?"

"Arrogance," Marcus huffs.

I meet Laney's eyes, trying to control my laughter. "I don't think Luna approves of your boyfriend."

"Luckily I don't need her approval," he snaps. "Or yours."

"Oh? I could cause more problems than you want to—"

"That's enough," Laney whines. "You guys are ruining tonight," she whispers, picking up her plate. She makes her way to the living room, her shoulders looking a little saggier than normal.

"Stop being so confrontational, Alandra," Marcus sighs. "Can't you see what you do to her?"

"What *I* do to her?" I ask, my voice barely a whisper. I narrow my eyes on the piece of shit before me and sit my glass down on the table, ever so carefully. "You're bold, I'll give you that. I wonder how my poor sister is going to feel when she finds out you made a pass at me."

"I did not."

"Liar."

"Alandra, I—"

Slashing my hand through the air to silence him, I grab my wine glass and stand. I don't have to deal with this shit. Taking a play from Luna's book, I remove myself from the situation and head toward my room. Marcus is a liar but he's right, I can't prove any of it. And that's exactly why I had decided to let all of this go. Something about his behavior tonight set my nerves on edge, though. It made it hard to remember why I'd chosen to behave myself in the heat of the moment. I sigh and shake my head, hovering outside my bedroom door for a moment longer than necessary.

I'm a little nervous to enter my own damn bedroom. I know *she's* in there and it's intimidating. Sure, there'd been some mild flirtation between the two of us, but the dream I'd had changed things in my mind, somehow. It shifted my perception of her from other, to very, very real. And now I can't keep my mind off exactly how very, very real she is.

Chapter 11
Alandra

Luna skips ahead of me toward an elderly witch on the side of the street. I can't remember the woman's name, but she's known for peddling useless trinkets to tourists. Some of her stuff is good, though, if you know what you're looking for. That's the problem, however, tourists *never* know what they're looking for.

"Oh, braidbrooms!" Luna seems absolutely giddy and I can't discern why as I approach the two of them. Her hands wrap firmly around a cheap straw broom that reeks of cinnamon and I roll my eyes.

The only thing these are good for is placing by the back door of the house. They draw financial energy, supposedly. Our mother used one religiously growing up, but we never struck it rich, so I'm not a big believer.

"Yes ma'am," the woman coughs. I narrow my eyes on her, unsure if she's trying to gain sympathy from a would-be victim or if she's actually ill. The woman covers her mouth and her shoulders shake through the coughing spell. Nope, that's legit. She's sick.

"Why haven't you seen a healer?" Luna asks, sitting the broom down against the small table of trinkets.

"I don't have the money and nothing worth trading right now," she admits. Her grey hair falls into her face and I'm struck with a strong sense of shame. I can't believe I was judging her a few seconds ago. This woman had obviously had a hard life.

Luna clicks her tongue against her teeth and shoos away the moth flitting around her head. "Not now, Beezlebub."

I make a quiet *pss pss pss* sound with my mouth to draw Beezlebub's attention. He hovers above my shoulder but refuses to sit down as we both watch Luna cup the cheeks of the older woman.

"What are you—"

"Shh," Luna pleads. "This will only take a moment."

The old woman's eyes meet mine, full of fear and anticipation. I smile apologetically at her. There's not much else I can do, since I don't know what's happening either. I trust Luna, though.

Power brushes against me and a shiver runs down my spine. Whatever Luna is doing requires a decent amount of energy. Her eyebrows cinch together and her mouth moves but no sound comes out. Beezlebub lights onto my shoulder, creeping underneath my hair. I can empathize with him, the power radiating from Luna is ridiculous.

A few people walking by stop to stare. I don't know most of them, probably humans come to get their trendy witchy relics. I hazard a step toward Luna; I know I have to get her to stop before she exposes herself. I'm not entirely sure what she's doing—some kind of healing, I'd guess—but it's drawing too much attention.

"Do not interfere," she hisses without looking away from the old woman.

My mouth crinkles into a grimace and I stop in my tracks. I know better than to piss the Celestial off, if nothing else. The woman sways in her cheap, pop up seat. Color seems to be filling her, life radiating from her once frail looking body.

"Luna, you've done it," I whisper.

"Almost," she replies before returning to her silent chant.

"What's happening?" someone asks and I turn to send them on their way then quickly realize I'm face to face with Jess.

My mouth falls open as my heart does a tiny somersault. I'm not proud of the excitement that rushes through me when I see her. Her beanie—the one I bought her last year—is lopsided as usual and her nose is pink from the cold.

"What are you doing here?"

"Visiting," she begins. "I was going to come see you, but you wouldn't take my calls so I just—"

"Oh." I scrunch my nose up and look back to Luna, who is brushing her hands along the sides of the jacket I'd insisted she wear if we were going into town.

"Yeah. I um—how have things been?" Jess's big brown eyes bore into me and I have to remind myself not to squirm.

I have to remind myself I'm not doing anything wrong by ignoring her calls. Our relationship ended, I don't have to make myself available to her anymore, but it's hard to remember that when she's standing in front of me looking self-conscious.

"Good. Work has been busy, I guess."

"That's great!"

"Yeah," I agree as the old woman jumps to her feet, her hand on her chest.

"Oh my Goddess, thank you. Thank you, Angel, thank you." She throws her arms around Luna and then takes off down the sidewalk, completely abandoning her little display of sellable goods

"Who's your friend?" Jess asks, narrowing her eyes on Luna.

"Luna."

"Well, I can see why you haven't been returning my calls," she sniffs, turning to leave.

"Fuck you, man. You left me here. You took an amazing job and I'm super fucking happy for you but don't you dare come here and accuse me of anything like you have the right." My cheeks and chest warm with the anger spreading through me. She has some nerve to try to call me out for something I'm well within my rights to do. Something I'm not even doing.

"Woah, I just—"

"No," I snap, holding up my hand. "I don't want to hear it. You left. You don't get to show up jealous just because you see me with a beautiful woman. You don't get to guilt trip me for moving on with my life and leaving you in the past."

"You told me to take the job!" she yells, throwing her hands in the air. "What the hell do you want from me?"

"I told you to take the job because it was right for *you*," I whisper.

"it was never going to be right for me. That doesn't mean you shouldn't do it. I *am* happy for you. I'm proud, too, but it doesn't change the fact that we can't be together now and we both need to move on."

"That's easier for some of us than others, I guess," Jess growls.

"Have a Blessed Yule, Jess." I turn and march down the sidewalk, shaking my head as I go.

"It's *Merry Christmas* for humans!" Jess screams behind me and I actually laugh as I continue walking away. Does she really think I don't know the difference?

The sound of footsteps and the soft buzz of magic follow me as I head toward the herbalist.

I mumble under my breath, I'm not even sure it's English that comes out. It's cold out. The sidewalk is slippery. My ex is in town and somehow I'm the bad guy. I have to keep Luna's identity a secret until she can go home to her realm and I'm not mentally, emotionally, or magically prepared for any of this fuckery today.

Chapter 12
Luna

My eyes widen as I watch Alandra point her finger at the girl before storming off.

"It's *Merry Christmas* for humans!" she screams, stomping her feet. Her blue and pink hair has me narrowing my eyes. This is the girl from Alandra's dreamscape.

The cruel one.

As I move to follow the Little Witch, the human steps in front of me, narrowing her eyes. My eyebrow arches and I glance around at the people moving past us on the sidewalk. A few had been interested while I was healing the old woman, but it seemed their fascination stopped as soon as the magic did.

How typical.

"Can I help you?" I ask when she doesn't speak.

"Yeah. Who the fuck are you?"

My eyebrows shoot into my hairline and it takes every ounce of patience I've cultivated over the eons not to fling this mortal into traffic for speaking to me in such a way.

"I'm Luna. And you are?"

"Jess." She bites her bottom lip, tears welling in her light brown eyes. "How do you know Landra?"

"Alandra? We . . . just met." My eyes flick away from this Jess and down the sidewalk where Alandra is quickly moving out of my sight.

"I—I miss her," she whispers quietly. "I'm sorry for being rude." Her candor shocks me and I turn to face the thin woman with a nod.

"I understand. Relationships are messy and hard. I don't have much experience with them myself, but—" I shake my head. I'm saying too much. I don't want to give myself away to this mortal. A quote that drifted to me in my own realm drifts across my mind now and I smile sadly at the girl. "Sometimes, things just aren't meant to be."

"I hope you two are happy." She wipes at her eyes and turns away from me, walking down the street with her head hung low.

I want to correct her, tell her that me and the Little Witch aren't in a relationship. I want to set the facts straight and be honest with the human, but something in my chest won't let me.

No, something in my chest is urging me, even now, to turn around and follow Alandra to make sure she's safe. To go wrap my arms around her and hold her so tightly that all of her broken pieces fit back together.

And that's exactly what I'm going to do. I cast one last look at the human walking off into the distance before I turn to look for my Little Witch. I don't know what I can offer her. I know I can't stay in this realm forever, even when the magic keeping me here wears off with the solstice, and I have a choice in the matter again. I'll have to return to my own realm.

My eyes drift over the heads of people in front of me, searching out the platinum haired witch I'm looking for. I think I see her disappear around a corner when a hand comes down on my wrist.

I look first at the hand that dares to touch me, then my eyes raise up to the face attached to such a stupid limb.

"You're coming with me," he growls, jerking me into a narrow space between two buildings.

My eyes go wide, but my heart doesn't beat with fear. No, it beats with anger. I snatch my arm free from the mortal's grasp, my power gathering around me.

"I'm going to leave and you're not going to follow me." I turn to my left, to exit the small alleyway and find myself surrounded by shadow, unable to see through it. The only thing visible is me and my would-be attacker.

"You don't want to do this," I plead with him, my hand drawing up as my eyes narrow on his hand. He holds a dark colored sack with a drawstring at the opening. Even from here, I can feel the magic wafting from here. It's spelled.

"We've been looking for you, Celestial." The mortal shakes the bag by his hip and takes a step toward me, a sinister smile playing across his face. "Lucky for me I just so happened to see you heal the old crone on the sidewalk. And what were you doing with that pretty little null, anyway?" He takes another step. "She's a pretty thing, but she's got all the power of a goldfish."

My mouth goes dry at the mention of Alandra. He knows what I am and he saw me with my Little Witch.

I take a deep breath and curl my fingers in toward my palm, pulling on the water inside the mortal's body. He stops in his tracks, his eyes going wide as water pours out from the pores all over his body. I shake my hand, wishing it didn't have to be this way.

"I'm sorry," I whisper, before clenching my hand into a fist. The man falls to his knees but they never meet the ground. He explodes into a puddle of water and goop. My nose wrinkles as the smell hits me. The shadows secluding us in the narrow alleyway fall as his magic dissipates back into the ether from which it came.

With a shudder, I step over the pile of skin and bones in the middle of a bloody water puddle. I need to find Alandra. I look out into the busy sidewalk to see if the mortals had any idea about what transpired.

Just as I thought, they didn't seem to have a clue. The shadow caster had blanketed us in magic, keeping the outside world completely separate during our little encounter.

I swipe my hands down the front of my dress as I begin walking in the direction Alandra had gone. I need to find her and check on her. And maybe tell her about the dead witch who tried to kidnap me.

Chapter 13

Alandra

Glancing around, I realize that I've walked much farther than I intended. Main street thins out toward this end, changing from little shops and restaurants to doctor offices and insurance agents. I let out a frustrated sigh and turn around, nearly colliding with Luna.

"Sorry," she whispers, placing a steadying hand on my shoulder.

"It's okay." I go to move but her grip holds me firmly in place, forcing me to meet her eyes.

"No, it isn't," she murmurs. She doesn't move. She doesn't say anything else. She just stands there, looking at me as if she actually sees me and something about that breaks me apart inside.

"I'm so fucking tired of being the bad guy all the time," I whimper, my eyes brimming with unexpected tears.

Luna wraps her arms around me and pulls me close to her. Her hand on the back of my head guides my cheek to her shoulder. "I know."

"No, it's all the time. Everything. Everyone. I'm not good enough. My family barely tolerates me. Jess left but she's mad at *me*. I fucked up your life temporarily, too—"

Her lips pressing against the side of my head cuts me off. Luna shakes her head, squeezing me tighter. "It was inconvenient, yes. But in truth, I was lonely there. The companionship has been nice. You aren't the bad guy."

Sniffling against her chest like some kind of emotionally deranged child, I stand there and soak up those words. At least one person in the world doesn't think I'm a burden. Granted, that person isn't even from this world... but semantics.

"Thank you," I whisper.

Her hands rub my back through my coat and a happy sigh slips past my lips. We stand like that for I don't know how long, just wrapped up in the moment until I notice the sun starting to set.

"Shit!"

"What's wrong?"

"The herbalist is traditional. She'll close before the sun sets," I groan, reluctantly backing out of the hug before I begin power walking toward the herbalist shop. "If I don't get the ingredients on the list, my mom will flay me."

"Well, that would be unfortunate," Luna laughs as she hurries to catch up to my side. She laces her fingers through mine with a precision that makes me question this so-called loneliness she claims to experience in her realm.

But instead of asking, I just squeeze her fingers in mine and walk faster. *Tonight is going to be interesting.*

"I need to tell you something," Luna adds in a meek voice as we make our way down the sidewalk.

"What's up?"

"When you left, a man pulled me into the alley and tried to attack me." Her voice is quiet and I glance at her face, my feet planting firmly on the sidewalk as she pulls slightly ahead.

"Do what now?"

"He knew what I am. And he threatened me. He threatened you." Luna's lip trembles just the slightest bit and I throw my arms around her neck again, squeezing her tight.

"Why wouldn't you tell me this right away?!" My voice sounds frantic, even to me. She just shrugs in my arms.

"You were upset. I wanted to make sure you were okay first. Alandra," her voice tapers off with a heavy sigh as she presses her nose into my hair. "He knew what I am. There are dark witches in your Waitsfield."

I blink. She's right.

"Someone came after you," I repeat the words again, the implication really setting in. "Fuck. Luna, I'm so sorry. I don't know what I can—"

Luna presses her fingertips to my lips, silencing me before tugging on my hand to continue our walk to the herbalist. "It's not your fault, Little Witch. I handled it."

"What do you mean you *handled* it?" I narrow my eyes on her, wondering—not for the first time—precisely what this woman is capable of.

"He threatened us both. I can protect myself, but I can't let anyone come after you."

"What did you do, Luna?" I ask as we near the small shop.

"He won't be a problem for anyone anymore," she whispers, her eyes falling to the ground as if ashamed. I suck in a breath and nod, trying to hear what I already know. Luna can be dangerous.

"Hey, look at me," I finally whisper as we take the first step onto the stairs that lead into the store. "You did what you had to do."

Luna smiles at me and nods, her white hair flowing around her face with the gesture. I shake my hand and open the door to the shop. Before I step in, I cast a worried glance around behind us, convinced a dark witch would pop out at any moment.

It was going to be an interesting night, indeed.

Chapter 14
Unknown

I nudge the pile of soup covered bones with the toe of my shoe and nearly gag. The smell is atrocious. This isn't my first time dealing with remains, but it is by far the worst.

"What happened to him?" my partner asks, covering her mouth. We'd been paired together when I joined this sect of The Order. Agreeing to working with her had been the single stupidest thing I'd ever done. The woman is a beauty, and I'm very much married.

I swallow, pushing away the memories of past mistakes. We only work together now. She knows that and judging by sweat beading on her brow in the middle of December, she has other concerns at the moment.

"Liquified? He called and said he thought he'd found the Celestial. I told him not to go after it alone."

"That surge earlier? Everyone in Waitsfield felt it."

"Yeah, that's the one. He said he was pretty sure he knew who caused it and hung up. Fucking idiot. He could still be alive if his ego hadn't gotten in the way." I shake my head and turn to leave the alley.

Behind me, bright light flashes repeatedly until she comes to my side once again. Wrapping her arm around my back. "All gone," she murmurs.

"Stop that, we're in public," I hiss. "And you know I'm married."

"You've been married the whole time I've known you," she laughs. "Never stopped you before."

I shrug out of her hold and pick up the pace as I dig my cell phone out of my jacket pocket. Someone needs to let the coven leader know what's happened.

How did I get so lucky?

Chapter 15
Alandra

I pull my legs underneath my butt and snuggle deeper into the couch. The fire roaring in the living room reminds me of when we were kids. I used to lay here and watch Laney draw on the floor during the snowstorms that always seem to wreak havoc on Waitsfield during Yule.

"It's like the Yule our ancestors experienced," my mom would say. "They'd be stuck inside during the long, cold nights, and spend the time telling stories with their families and eating dried foods they'd prepared for winter." I'm just glad we don't have to rely on dried meats and canned vegetables anymore.

That would put a serious kink in my holiday festivities.

"Whatcha doing?" Laney asks from behind the couch. I nearly jump, throwing a hand over my chest to steady the rapid beat growing there.

"I was just thinking about our childhood," I admit. "It was easier back then."

"It was," she sighs. "Where's Luna?"

"She went outside. I think she's homesick, even though she won't admit it."

Laney nods slowly, her hand fidgeting mercilessly with the hair at the nape of her neck. "How are you holding up? I heard what happened in town earlier."

"Luna told you?"

"Yeah."

"I'm fine," I lie. I'm definitely not fine. In fact, this nostalgic ass mood is probably all because of the drama in town earlier. But that's fine. Now isn't the time to think about that. Now it's time to deal with my insane family and pray we get through this dinner without any massive blow ups.

If Dad is having another affair, that probably won't happen. But we'll see.

"You ready?"

"Yeah," I yawn, stretching my arms over my head. The fire is cozy and makes me want to lie on the couch all night long, but that isn't going to happen. I jump to my feet, intent on waking up a little bit more, when the back door opens and a gust of cold air slaps me in the face.

"Shit!" I snap, rubbing my hands across my bare arms. I quickly pull my hoodie from the couch and shove my head through it. The sound of a door clicking shut rings through the living room, but I already know who it is.

Even if I hadn't known she was outside, I'd know who it is just by the power rolling through the room as she moves through it. Luna is a fucking force of nature.

And I have no idea what I'm going to tell my parents.

Oh shit.

"You ready?" I ask her, trying to mask my own nervousness.

Luna slips her hand in mine and nods. "It will be fun, I'm sure."

Laney's eyes drop to the linked fingers between us and then raise to meet mine. "I see you've been working on your cover story."

"Well," I laugh. "Cousins wouldn't exactly work with them."

"True." Laney blows out a puff of air, opens her mouth as if she wants to say something, then ruffles her hair with her hand and walks off.

"I don't think she approves," Luna murmurs as we make our way to the kitchen behind Laney.

"She's not a fan of any bad decisions but her own." Truer words had never been spoken, but I can't believe I actually said them out loud.

"Wow," Laney huffs, spinning around to confront me. "You're turning into a real bitch lately."

"I am not, I just—"

"What's going on here?" Dad asks from the table, laying down his newspaper. Who actually reads newspapers anymore? Everything is digital. I'm surprised they still deliver them. He's one of those people who would riot if they stopped, though. He loves going into rants about how technology, the greatest innovation of man, has killed innovation in general. It's all very sophisticated and kind of boring, if I'm honest.

I enjoy modern convenience.

"Nothing," Laney snaps, narrowing her eyes on me in a final display of her unhappiness. That'll be fun to deal with later. Not.

"Mmhm," he grumbles. A growl echoes nearby and I instantly search for Diego. That wolf is always setting off my alarm bells. Laney claims it's because I have a passive familiar. Judging by the angry chittering coming from Beezlebub on the wall, I don't think he's very passive, but maybe that's just me.

"Whatever." Laney marches the rest of the way to the table and sits down in her seat. She's mad, but what I said wasn't that bad and it happens to be true. She's made some pretty fucked up decisions in her life. Not least of all being her taste in partners.

Mom glides from the stove to the kitchen, or at least it looks like she glides. The billowing black dress adds to the effect. "Sit down, girls, everything's ready."

I squeeze Luna's hand in mine before I make my way to my cramped seat. She takes the empty seat next to Laney, who's still glaring daggers in my direction.

Mom sets a few more pots in the center of the table then takes her seat. With a smile, she turns to Luna, "And who is this? You girls disappeared the moment you came in! I haven't even gotten an introduction."

"Oh, I'm sorry Mom," I cough, sitting straighter in my seat. I gesture toward Luna, trying not to blush. "This is Luna, my girlfriend." That was the agreed upon lie. The cousins routine obviously wouldn't work with my parents, so we had come up with this idea.

Luna agreed to go along with it, and something about her lack of shock about the plan was unnerving.

"It's very nice to meet you, Mrs. Michaels."

"A new girlfriend, hm? Well, at least this one is a witch." Dad slops a serving of green bean casserole onto his plate then quickly begins picking through the slices of ham. "It's nice to meet you, Luna."

"Please, call me Audrey," Mom murmurs before her head cocks to the side. I know she's being harassed by some needy spirit, but it still looks rude.

"And I'm Sterlen," Dad adds with a gruff nod.

I try not to focus on the witch comment and instead begin loading my own plate down with vegetables and ham. Luna doesn't like meat, but at least she has the sides to choose from.

"Where did you two meet?" Mom asks, finally checking back into the conversation just as Luna spoons an extra portion of squash onto her plate.

"How else? Bug fucked up our shopping for the blessing—"

"Laney!" Dad snaps. "I will not tolerate rudeness in front of guests."

"Or at all, for that matter," Mom adds with a glare. "That language is unnecessary, young lady."

It's hard not to point out that neither of us are that young, but I manage to keep it to myself. Luna looks even paler than normal, if that's possible. I know she's probably uncomfortable. The tension in this house has always been unbearable, well at least for me.

"Well, at least you two are finally on the same side," Laney mutters before taking a bite of ham.

"Laney Eileen," Mom hisses. My eyes fly to Dad's and I can see the annoyance brewing there. Beezlebub darts under the table, braving Diego to sit on my thigh. He knows they don't like to see him at the table, it tends to gross people out, but I appreciate the closeness right now.

"She's right, though," I sigh. "I forgot a few things and then the shop was closed. I got online looking for another herbalist and I found one." I glance away from them, toward Luna, and find her smiling at me. If I didn't know any better, I'd say she believed the lie herself.

"It couldn't have worked out more perfectly," Luna purrs.

Dad narrows his eyes, glancing between the two of us. I can tell he has something else to add, but for now he's keeping it himself. I wonder for a moment if he's tempted to comment on Luna's power. If her strength is obvious to me, it must slap the rest of my family in the face.

The dinner fades into a comfortable silence as everyone eats, only interrupted by the occasional question about how work is going. Laney seems to have calmed down some. I wish I could make her see things from my perspective, but she'll have to learn on her own. Being the big sister is hard sometimes. I want to fix everything for her but at the same time, I know I can't. I'm not her keeper.

I've always hated those stupid placards. I am *not* my sister's keeper. I am not responsible for her shitty decisions or her welfare. I want her to be safe and do great things and make the best of all the opportunities she has available to her, but she has to be the one to take those steps. All I can do is point to them and suggest it, and I can only do that so many times before it's pointless.

"These green beans are delicious," Luna coos from her seat, wiping at the corner of her mouth. "Honestly, they're divine."

"Well, thank you, Luna."

Luna smiles warmly at my mother but she's already engaged in some whispered conversation with a spirit. I wish she could turn her power off and be fully present for once. Maybe I should be thankful it's one less set of eyes prying at the lie.

"What about your family, Luna? Who are they?" Dad leans back in his chair, his plate empty, and laces his fingers together against his stomach.

This is what I was hoping to avoid. These questions. *Why did I think it would be a good idea to bring her here?*

"I'm a solitary witch," Luna lies effortlessly. "My family is distant compared to this close knit group you have here."

"Ah, that must be hard." Dad leans forward, obviously interested and I try not to cringe.

"You're awfully powerful for a solitary witch. Most witches draw more power from their coven, have you ever considered joining one?"

"Why would I do that? I have all I need."

"You could contribute to something bigger than yourself—"

"Dad! She's happy with her own practice, let her be." I push my plate away, narrowing my eyes on him.

"It's not like you'd understand what I mean, Alandra. Have you ever felt the surge of power when practicing when other witches? I know it's different for you." The last words are meant to soften the blow, but the effect is the same. He's putting me in my place and wants me to know it. I'm *'practically a null'* and shouldn't comment on other witches' practice. My fingers curl into my palm and I look away from him, trying to brush off the slight.

"It's alright, Alandra. We know you have your own value," Mom murmurs before taking a sip of tea.

"Honestly, I wish you would take those classes to be an herbalist. That way you can at least explore your potential as a green."

"I'm not a green." My lips tighten even as I speak the words for the millionth time in my life.

"You could be, if you applied yourself," Dad notes. "There's nothing wrong with being a green. You'd be more in tune with your magic, maybe something would spark in you that could be useful." He scrunches his nose up then adds, "magically, of course."

Laney fidgets in her seat and I set my vision on her as I try to drown out the usual rant. She shrugs her shoulders apologetically. "Bug is happy doing her music."

"And we're happy for you, baby, truly," Mom adds in a too-sweet tone. "We just worry you're not reaching your full potential."

Beezlebub crawls up my thigh until he's resting on my stomach, wings spread out like some kind of ancient, ornate brooch. His quiet chittering settles my nerves a little. At least he gets it.

"Why does her profession matter so much? I don't understand." Luna takes a sip of her tea, glancing curiously between everyone at the table.

"Well, if you aren't close with your family, you probably wouldn't understand." Dad's tone leaves no room for argument, but Luna persists.

"Shouldn't a good family want you to be happy?"

"We want great things for our children, that's not a crime," he snaps.

"Alandra has always been a little different, Luna. You may not understand, honestly, since you have so much magic inside you. Your energy has been filling the house since you arrived. Alandra has so little, though, in comparison. We just want her to have a fulfilled life. It's hard to be a witch with no affinity." Mom smiles weakly at me. She means well and I know she does, but her words still sting.

"Maybe comparing her is the problem. She has more value than I think you give her credit for," Luna adds, tilting her head to the side as if confused.

"It's fine, Luna—"

"No. Why do they all treat you like you're less?" She turns toward my dad and engages him fully. "She can question other witches' practice as often as she feels like. She *is* a witch, even if she doesn't have an active power like you."

"I think I know how to handle my own daughter." Dad's face flushes red. He's never been able to handle having his authority questioned. A growl rumbles beneath the table and I swallow hard. I've always hated that wolf. He's tried to eat Beezlebub more times than I can count and even went after Juniper once. Luckily, Juney is big enough to defend herself and made sure he'd never try to fuck with her again.

"Then treat her like a proper being and not some extension of your own egotistical need for power," Luna hisses, her back straightening in her seat.

Just as Dad opens his mouth to speak again, it feels like all the air in the room is sucked out, vented into space somewhere. My skin breaks out in goosebumps and Beezlebub clambers up my body until he can rest against my neck, facing the brewing drama. A high pitched whine beneath the table pierces my ears.

"I think you should calm down, dear," Mom whispers, her eyes skirting around the room to things the rest of us can't see.

"I think we should leave." I press my chair back into the wall and slide out from my spot with a severity I didn't know I had in me. "Blessed Yule, everyone," I murmur, brushing past Dad.

"Alandra, wait," he sighs. "You don't have to go." He points to Luna and shakes his head. "And you have some nerve threatening me in my own home. I wouldn't dare use magic against a guest, but you are no longer welcome here." His head tilts back with a self-righteous sniff.

"Blessed Yule," I ground out again, moving away from the table. A movement from Mom catches my eye. Her eyes are wide, brimming with tears. I don't think anyone has ever called them out for how they treat me before. It's a strange mix of gratifying and upsetting.

Luna nods her head slowly, never breaking eye contact with my father, before she pushes her chair back and begins to follow me. I turn my back on the dinner, heading toward the door but a small bit of conversation causes me to pause near the exit.

"You should be more careful, Luna," Mom says between tears. "That's a lot of power here. Even if it doesn't seem like it."

The hairs on the back of my neck prickle but I try to shake the eerie feeling that my mom already knows who—and what—Luna is. That's a problem for another day. Besides, she'll be gone soon.

"Thank you, Audrey. Blessed Yule."

Stepping out into the cold, whipping wind, I hustle toward my car. It's too cold and I'm in the world's worst mood. I don't want to deal with *any* of this. I just want to get home, curl up in my blanket, and work on some music. I've been distracted lately—for obvious reasons—and I need to get my work back in order. Luckily, my clients understand I'm hard to reach during holidays and don't send me anything pressing this time of year.

As I slide into the car, Luna opens the passenger door and sits down. She closes it gently, then folds her hands in her lap. "I apologize."

"For what?" I ask as I crank the car. Usually I'd let it warm up before I start driving, but fuck that. Fuck that with a cactus. I just want to get as far away from here as possible right now.

"I'm sure I made things worse," she whispers. I glance at her before I turn out into the street and notice the way her head hangs, staring down into her lap.

"No." I shake my head. "Thank you."

"Thank you?"

"Yes, thank you. No one has ever stood up for me to them. It's so fucking hard being the only Michaels with no affinity. Hell, I'm the only person in Waitsfield with no affinity. It's like everyone here is extraordinary and then you have me, normal little Alandra."

"You're not normal," she corrects me, trying to sound supportive, but I just bust out laughing.

"Are you calling me weird?"

"Weird?"

"Abnormal." I snort and cover my mouth as I merge into traffic. I'm not sure why there's so many people out and about right now. Shouldn't everyone be at home with their families, feasting?

Luna screws her face up as she considers that. "Aren't witches considered abnormal in general? This realm was meant for humans."

I toss her a confused glance before I respond. "What do you mean it was meant for humans."

"Well, witches didn't originate here . . . surely you knew—"

"What?!" My head snaps toward her and my mouth falls open. I would have remembered *that* from my schooling, surely.

"Watch the road!" she squeals and my head snaps back forward just in time to slide to a stop at a red light.

"We aren't from here? Where do we come from then?"

"Um, I think we're getting off topic, here."

"Luna—"

"I just meant you aren't abnormal for a witch, is all. Stop thinking you are." She reaches a hand out and brushes some hair away from my face before tucking it behind my ear. "You're spectacular, Alandra."

My heart races in my chest as she traces icy fire along my neck. Everywhere her fingers meet skin, tiny little explosions fire along my nerves. It's unsettling, distracting. My neck shivers and the light turns green, signaling for me to start driving again, but it takes me a moment to react. The way Luna looks at me makes me feel . . . I don't really know the word for it.

It just makes me *feel*.

Chapter 16
Alandra

We walk to the door in silence. My phone buzzes in my pocket, but I ignore it. It can't be anything good and I don't want to hear any more negativity right now. With a sigh, I take it out and lay it face down on the little table near the door, then deposit my keys in the bowl beside it.

"What do you normally do to relax?" Luna asks, pushing the door shut.

"Make sure you lock it," I remind her. She nods and twists the lock until a satisfying thunk rings out. I nod and move toward the living room, grabbing the oversized knitted blanket I'd made last fall. It's gorgeous, but it's also super fucking comfortable and right now, I don't want it to be a decoration in the living room. I want to snuggle it.

"Hey, don't ignore me, Little Witch." Luna's voice cuts through the darkness and a shudder races down my spine. I didn't turn the lights on when we came in. Something in me wants to run from her, ignore the power in her voice, shut myself in my room, and just cry until I break apart into a new person.

But I can't do that.

"I usually turn on some music and just vibe until I don't remember why I was upset anymore," I admit quietly as I pull the blanket around my shoulders.

Luna stands there, the slight glow from her skin barely illuminating the space between us. Her face is passive and I hate that I have no idea what she's thinking. She stood up for me, but what if she realized how useless I am?

Well, surely she knows. I did fuck up a simple spell to bring her here. With that sobering thought, I turn toward my bedroom and kick off my shoes in the general direction of the kitchen.

"Do you want me to stay out here?" she asks quietly.

"No."

I should say yes. I know I should say yes. Nothing good is going to come from her watching me break down, but I don't want to be alone right now. I don't want to feel isolated like I have felt my entire life. I don't bother turning on the hall light either, I just walk by memory until I finally reach my door. I walk in and curl up carefully on the bed.

My fingertips can just barely reach the Bluetooth speaker. It should connect to my phone even though I left it in the other room. I take a deep breath, press play, then pull my arm back underneath the blanket and close my eyes.

The bed sags with the weight of another person, but I ignore her.

"I want you to feel better, Alandra. I meant everything I said in the car."

"I know you did. I just don't know if you know better," I answer softly. Her words have been replaying over and over in my head, but instead of fixing the broken parts inside of me like I want them to, they just reinforce that I'm not good enough and somehow I've managed to trick this wonderful Goddess of a being into somehow believing I'm better than I am.

There's a word for it. I can't remember it right now, but I remember reading an article about it online. Some kind of syndrome where you feel like you've somehow weaseled your way into anything good you have. I'm fucking unreasonable. And I know that, but I just can't make it stop.

"You'd question me?" Luna shimmies under the blanket with me, wrapping an arm around my waist from behind. "Don't your people think the Celestials are some kind of Gods?"

"Aren't you?"

"Not exactly."

"I'm probably the last one to ask. I don't know if you've noticed," I laugh. "But I'm pretty much the worst witch ever."

Her fingers trace tiny patterns across my ribs as she hums against the back of my shoulder. "Is that so?"

"Yup. Don't have an affinity? Check." I fling out a finger for each self-deprecating fact as they come to mind. "Accidentally summoned the Moon? Check. Family hates you? Check."

"They don't hate you."

"They don't love me either," I whisper.

Luna slides the fingers of her other hand into my hair and begins massaging my scalp. I want to protest, I want to tell her 'No, I don't deserve to feel good.' But I'm selfish and her fingernails against my scalp feel like my own personal piece of Heaven.

"I don't think that's true," she murmurs against the bend of my neck where it meets my shoulder. Goosebumps race across my back and I bump back against her soft body. "I think they don't know how to love you *correctly.*"

My heart thuds in my chest as the intimacy of this moment washes over me. Laying in the dark, wrapped up in her arms, her warmth seeping into my body as I hide under my favorite blanket. It's one of those moments that only seem to happen in movies. At least for me.

"How can they love me correctly?" I'm scared to hear the answer, honestly. I'm not entirely sure what she means and I'm so close to breaking right now already, if she says something cruel I might fall apart. But maybe she means all the nice things she says. Maybe she's actually different. Maybe she can grant all the wishes I made on the moon over the years.

Luna props up on her elbow and rolls me toward her, forcing me to look up at her face. The soft light from her skin barely touches mine, it's such a faint radiance. She slides a hand down my cheek and smiles.

"By letting you be the best you that you can. There's no right way to exist, Alandra. They can love you correctly by loving your life."

I don't know if it's the sad smile that pulls at her lips when she speaks the words, or the way her inner light makes my heart lurch, or the feel of her silky fingers caressing my cheek, but I take a chance.

I lean up, slowly, and slide my hand into the hair at the base of her head. My breath hitches when her eyes slide shut, as if anticipating what comes next. My lips hover a breath away from hers for what feels like an eternity before I finally close the distance and press my mouth against hers. The kiss is soft at first, much like the first one we shared. Sipping at her lips slowly, I can feel all the weight on my shoulders slide away. With every breath, the heavy feeling in my stomach dissipates and turns into something different as she tilts her head to the side, deepening our kiss.

Luna's tongue plays across mine in a fluid motion which sends a shudder through me. Heat pools in my center as her hand slips from my face down my arm to my hip, and finally to my ass. When she pulls me against her, her fingers dig into my ass like she owns me, I whimper against her lips.

"Let me love you, Little Witch, at least while I can," Luna breathes against my mouth, the words barely a whisper.

A tiny piece of my heart breaks at those words. This can't last. This feeling, this completion I feel when her mouth is pressed against mine, her leg curving around my hip, her hands roaming my back as we breathe the same air . . . it can't last.

I blow out a breath of air, steeling my heart against the pain I know will come eventually, and nod.

Luna rolls us over without hesitation, plucking at my lips softly as she pushes my sweater up. She leans back long enough to pull it free over my head and I glance up at her with wide eyes, suddenly curious just how experienced this woman is.

"Stop worrying, love," she whispers with a smirk, as if reading my mind. I open my mouth to protest but her mouth closes around my nipple, through the thin material of my bralette. Oh. My. Fuck. The heat, even through the fabric, is almost enough to do me in.

My fingers twist through her shimmering hair until I realize there's way too many clothes between us. I sit up and Luna stumbles backward a bit, chuckling as I hastily pull my bra off over my head. I lean forward, my fingers bunch in Luna's borrowed dress as my lips crash against hers.

I need this.

I need her.

Her tongue brushes against my bottom lip and a whimper claws against the back of my throat as she presses her body against mine. I pull at the dress, trying to untangle it from her. Luna leans back and pulls it over her head in one easy motion. I can't help but stare.

"Fucking Goddess. You're beautiful," I murmur as I take the beautiful curves in front of me. Of course she wasn't wearing a bra . . . or panties, I note, as my eyes travel down the swell of her breasts to the patch shimmering curls between her thighs. My mouth waters and I lean forward again, my hands clinging to her waist as my mouth traces across her collarbone and down her chest.

Her nipples are perfect, begging for attention. When my tongue flicks out to tease one, my fingers close around the other, rolling it between my forefinger and my thumb until she squirms against me.

"Alandra," she whimpers. "Let me—"

"Shhh," I whisper against her breast, sliding my free hand down her smooth stomach to wet folds waiting for me. I gently slide a finger over her entrance, dragging the wet up to her clit and begin circling it. Luna's head rolls against her shoulders, her fingers twining through my hair as she rocks against my hand.

I lean back far enough to watch her face, twisting my hand so my thumb rolls over her clit as I slowly work a finger into her core. Her lips part on a breathy moan, her teeth grazing her bottom lip as her eyes open just enough to meet mine. I push her backward, gently, and slide another finger inside her as her head hits the mattress.

"Oh Great Goddess," she whispers in the dark. The need in her voice combined with her hips rolling up to meet my hand is so fucking perfect. Bending down, I brush my lips over hers, curling my fingers against the soft, pulsing flesh just inside her.

I lean down, dragging my tongue from her neck down her chest. I circle her nipple once, but barely breathe across the bud itself before moving lower, tracing a path down her stomach as I work my fingers in and out of her wet pussy.

My mouth hovers against her hip for a moment before I bite it gently, drawing a gasp from Luna. Her hips buck against my hand and I slam my fingers inside with a punishing intensity.

"Alandra," she moans, fisting her hands in the sheet.

Grinning against her skin, I kiss my way across the top of her pussy, teasing her with what we both know is coming. All the while, my fingers push deeper, stroking new places inside her.

I don't know what I expected to happen when I slid my tongue between her folds for the first time, but the jolt of energy that shocks me is beyond anything I've ever experienced. It's pure magic buzzing through me as I twist my tongue around her clit in exquisite little circles.

"Fuck, you taste amazing," I purr against her wet flesh, shivering as another hit of whatever magic is coursing through her rolls through my system.

Luna's fingers scrabble frantically for purchase against my scalp. Her core quivers around my fingers and I suck her swollen clit into my mouth, twirling my tongue against it as I push my fingers deeper inside her. Harder.

"Alandra!" she squeaks out and I can't help but think what a cute little mousey sound that is as her body shudders against me. I lap at her clit, long, even strokes as my fingers slow inside her, drawing the last waves of her orgasm with me before I lean up, wiping the back of my hand across my mouth. Luna's chest rises and falls as she recovers, her fingers pulling at my shoulders.

I slide up beside her and slip my hand into her hair before I brush my lips over hers. "What was that?" I ask, leaning my forehead against hers.

"What? Describe it," she murmurs, slipping her hand across my shoulder to wrap around my neck.

"Like magic, pulsing into me when I tasted you. It was bizarre," I laugh. "In a good way."

Luna hides her face in my neck, chuckling quietly. "I'm a Celestial, love," she whispers against the tender flesh just below my ear. "Sex and magic have a relationship older than even the Great Goddess can attest to, you can't separate the two. There's a reason that humans call it 'making love', or at least they used to. It's because two people create something when they join together, whether they mean to or not.

That's magic." Her tongue slides across my skin and all the heat that's been pooling in my core threatens to explode.

"That—that makes sense," I whisper as another shiver takes hold of my body. Luna's lips tickle my skin as she grins. I can't see it, but I can feel it.

"I'm glad you approve of the truth." She kisses her way across my neck to the hollow of my throat then bites down gently, just enough to send a zing of excitement through me. "I've never understood how one could try to separate sex, magic, and divinity. It's all the same. This world was born from it and only continues to survive because of a woman's pleasure." Her voice is hypnotic. My eyes roll back as she palms my tit, kissing her way across my chest.

Suddenly I'm reminded how tied the moon is to fertility magic and it makes sense. *But I have to say, this is the best lecture I've ever been a part of.*

Luna's breath tickles my thigh and a sharp pang of anxiety rockets through me. Did I shave this morning? How in the fuck can I expect her to go down on me after I know how *amazing* she tastes? I'm not a Celestial. I'm a witch. Practically a human. She tastes like fucking moonlight and I taste like . . . well, sex. I scrunch my nose up. I've tasted myself before, and it's not unpleasant, but it definitely isn't anything like—

Luna slides her tongue between my lips, the tip dancing from my entrance to my clit and every thought leaves my mind. My anxiety slips through my fingers and falls away when hers slide inside me.

"Shhh," she whispers against my pussy. "No thinking. Just feel." Her finger dips inside me, shallow at first, testing, then she surges deep into my core and my hands fly to her hair.

"Oh Goddess," I whimper when she pulls back and adds a second finger. She chuckles against my pussy before lapping from her fingers to my clit, slowly, deliberately, over and over. It's excruciating. The difference in pace sets my nerves on fire.

Her fingers dive in and out of my pussy, over and over again, building pressure deep in my core.

Her tongue laps slowly from my entrance to my clit.

I'd ask her how she can keep up the two different paces so consistently but I'm dumb. I can't speak. My brain is fucking broken, caught on some loop my neurons deemed pleasurable. That's the only explanation.

My hips arch off the bed of their own volition, grinding against Luna's mouth, chasing the friction I need. With a firm hand, she pushes my ass back down onto the bed, growling softly against me. "No."

Something about that no does terrible—or amazing—things to my insides. She resumes her torture. My orgasm is just out of reach, just on the other side of her terrible, amazing, fucking tongue.

Luna swirls the tip of her tongue around my clit in a circle and digs her free hand into my thigh. The change in pace and slight pinch of pain sends me over the edge. My fingers knot in her hair as my back arches and my legs start to tremble.

"Yes, fuck," I whimper as the first wave of pleasure courses through me.

Luna moans against my clit and curls her fingers into my g-spot and stars explode behind my lids. My hand falls from her hair as she sits up, still working her fingers slowly in and out of my pussy, drawing out every aftershock she can.

"Do you feel better, love?"

I snort and hold my hand out to her. She crawls up beside me and settles on her back. Laying my head on her chest, my leg across her hip, I blow out a heavy breath.

"Better is a word."

She chuckles and kisses my forehead softly, grinning against the skin. "Goodnight, Little Witch."

I blink, wondering if she really expects me to fall asleep right after that crippling orgasm, but suddenly, I realize she's right. My eyes are heavy and even her soft glow in the dark seems fuzzier than normal.

Goddess, I'm a lightweight.

Chapter 17
Luna

Something pulls me from the dreamscape and my mouth instantly squishes into what I'm sure is a fairly unattractive pout. The moon does not pout, but Alandra had been having an amazing dream—far better than the first one I'd witnessed in her mind—and something pulled me out of it.

Beezlebub hovers a few inches above my face and my eyebrow raises in question. "What is it?"

I glance to my right and find Alandra still asleep, her tousled hair spread out on the pillow above her head. She's so much more than she gives herself credit for. Beautiful, independent, strong willed. There needs to be more women like her in the world.

Beezlebub chitters, drawing my sleepy gaze back to him and away from the sleeping beauty beside me. I roll my eyes, and wave my hand at him. "Stop it, you pervert," I hiss.

Chitter.

A ping of anxiety and fear—not my own—washes through me and I jerk upright, glancing around the room. Nothing seems to be amiss. What in creation is he so upset about?

"What?" I ask again, as if he can answer me.

I close my eyes, sensing for magic around us, just to see if Laney made it home safely. Her pulsing light is nearby, in her bedroom. There's another pulse, too. Her boyfriend, maybe?

It's not until three more pulses light up the darkness of my mind that I begin to get nervous. This is what Beezlebub was trying to warn me about. There are people in the house.

People who don't belong here.

Panic shoots through me. I turn toward Alandra, shaking her until she begins to mumble. "Wake up, Little Witch," I rush out. "Something's very wrong."

"What? What is it?" she asks, rubbing her eyes.

"Is there any reason there'd be four extra people in the house at night?" I ask, hoping against hope that I'm wrong.

"What? No? Who's—"

Whatever Alandra was going to say gets cut off by the door slamming open. With the flick of a wrist, I slam it shut again, hopping to my feet. I'm nude, admittedly not the best position to be in when fighting adversaries, known or unknown, but something about fighting strangers naked seems even more off putting at the moment.

Someone strong is on the other side of the door, pushing at the barrier that's holding it closed. I quickly throw my dress on over my head and am pleased to see Alandra is already in her sweater. It's hardly long enough to keep her warm without pants, but there's no time. I point to the window and press my fingers to my lips.

The window raises as Alandra rushes toward it, grabbing a pair of shoes from beside her computer desk as she goes. Just as I make it to the other side of the bed, I feel the barrier break. These witches are strong.

It takes all four of them, but they manage to push past the barrier. When the door flies open this time, smoke immediately fills the room.

"B!" Alandra shrieks, the worry in her voice cutting through me like a knife.

I throw my hands up, coughing as the smoke fills my lungs. Alandra's coughs cut through the dense fog as well. Just as the magic leaves my palms to clear the smoke, a wave of dizziness hits me.

What in Creation . . .

"Run, Alandra," I gasp, covering my mouth and nose, but it's too late. I've already inhaled the valerian. Dropping to my knees, the last thing that crosses my mind before darkness fills my head is Alandra.

Valerian can be lethal to mortals. I'll end them.

Chapter 18
Alandra

My eyes blink open slowly, my head pounding. The faint light filtering through the window blinds me and I quickly shut my eyes again with a groan.

"Bug?" a familiar voice chokes out.

"Unghhh," I whimper, covering my eyes with my hand as I try to sit up.

"Slow down, you're still dosed." Laney lays a hand on my shoulder, steadying me as a million invisible pins and needles prick my skin all across my body. It's not as painful as it is annoying. I take inventory of my body and discover I'm okay aside from my limbs feel heavy and I'm having a hard time holding my eyes open.

"Dosed? Dosed with what?" I choke out on a cough.

"Valerian gas." Laney pushes my hair back from my face, her cool hand brushing against my forehead as she checks me over. "I was scared you wouldn't wake up. What happened?"

"I—" I shake my head, a huge mistake, and what little of my surroundings I can see swim away from me. Nausea rolls through my stomach. My eyes fly open, fighting to see through the tears the light causes. *I need to get to the bathroom.*

I blink away the tears, holding my stomach I try—and fail—to scramble to my feet. Laney's eyes go wide and she skitters backward as I lose my stomach on the bedroom floor.

As I'm caught in the disgusting puke cycle, flashes of what happened begin to slam into my mind one at a time until I remember.

Luna.

Laney hands me a wet wash rag and I wipe at my face and lean away from the mess on the floor. "They have Luna."

"Who? Who came for her?"

"I don't know. They knew we were here. How did they—" I groan again as another wave of nausea threatens me.

Laney scowls at me suspiciously before offering a glass of water I hadn't noticed she was holding. As I sip the cool liquid, Laney targets the pile of puke with her fire magic. I'd be worried about the flooring, but Laney is a prodigy. She has excellent control of her element. Before I'm through with my drink, there's nothing left on the floor except, well, floor.

"Nice trick," I mumble, setting the glass on the floor. I hold out a hand and Laney takes it, pulling me to my feet. "Witches came, I don't know who. They took her."

"You didn't see anything that could help?"

"No, I woke up to her telling me there were people in the house—" I narrow my eyes on Laney, a zing of panic racing down my spine. "Why aren't you sick?"

"They didn't come in my room. It was over by the time I woke up. Juniper never even growled."

I chew my lip, thinking that over. Laney's eyes narrow, clearly coming to the same conclusion as me. "Who wouldn't Juniper growl at?" I ask, rage settling in my stomach, forcing the last of the nausea away.

"That's a small list," Laney admits quietly, running a hand through her short hair.

With a growl, I pull some pants over my legs and adjust my sweater so it fits properly again. I march through the bedroom door, slamming it against the wall as I go. *That motherfucker.*

"Bug, wait! Where are you going?"

I round on Laney, anger simmering beneath my skin. "Who do we know who was both very interested in Luna, openly concerned with power, and whose new to Waitsfield?" I tick off every damning detail I can think of about Marcus.

"What? Who?" Laney's mouth clicks shut when she finally catches the accusation and she crosses her arms. "You think Marcus kidnapped Luna?"

"Who else could it be? The only people Juniper doesn't growl at are family and *your boyfriend.*" I roll my eyes. "Unless you kidnapped Luna? No? Then it was probably Marcus." I turn back around, leaving no room for debate with my asinine sister, and swipe my keys and cellphone from the table by the door.

"Juniper doesn't like Marcus—"

"And yet you still bring him around!" I snap. "Don't you think it should have been some kind of huge red flag that your *familiar*, the physical manifestation of your *magic*, doesn't like your boyfriend?" My fingers curl into my palms, my nails digging into the skin so hard I think they might bleed. "And she may not like him, but she's gotten used to his presence. I haven't heard her growl at him when she randomly encounters him."

"I have to lock her in the bedroom so she won't chew up his shoes!"

"But she does that happily, to annoy him and to make you see what a dumb fucking decision you're making," I accuse. "She doesn't growl at him.

"Are you coming with me or not?" I ask over my shoulder, the door already flying open as I yank on it.

"Yes," she squeaks. Laney hustles out the door behind me, pulling a coat over her shoulders.

A hot hand comes down on my shoulder as I reach the car and I spin around to face her. If I can feel the heat through my jacket, her magic is too close to the surface for her to be touching me and she knows it.

"He wouldn't do this. I know you don't like him, but he wouldn't do this. Please don't go over there accusing him. Can't we just . . . ask for his help and see how he reacts?"

Tilting my head to the side, considering her words, I slowly begin to nod. "Fine. That'll work, but the moment he says anything shady—"

Laney holds her hand up between us and nods. "If he did this, I'll broil him alive."

I swallow hard as the anger begins to dissipate and a crippling fear settles in my stomach. Someone *took* Luna. Someone took her and they are going to do terrible things to her if we didn't find her soon. I open the door to the car and meet Laney's eyes one last time before I slip inside.

"I can't lose her. Not like that."

"I know," she whispers, rubbing the top of my arm.

I nod, turning to the car and close the door behind me as I settle into the driver's seat. Luna doesn't deserve any of this. Images of her healing the old witch in town pass through my head and my head falls down on the steering wheel. She's a good person. She cares about people, even mortals like me who don't deserve her attention. She sees the good in me. I can't let anything happen to her.

I *won't* let anything happen to her. That thought echoes through my mind over and over until it's a soundtrack for my resolve. I'll find her and I'll put a stop to whatever bullshit those witches have planned for her.

MY PHONE DINGS IN MY POCKET AS WE APPROACH THE OVERSIZED entranceway of Marcus' home. Security cameras cling to the ceiling of the porch and I narrow my eyes on one as it twitches around to get a better view of us.

In moments, Marcus opens the door with a huge smile plastered on his face. "Baby!" He throws his arms around Laney and she hugs him awkwardly before stepping out of his embrace.

"Can we come in?"

"Of course," he answers, glancing nervously between the two of us. His eyebrow arches as I step past him and into the home, immediately looking around the large space. It wouldn't make sense for Luna to be kept somewhere so easily accessible, but I can't help but look anyway.

"What's up?" Marcus asks, heading toward the kitchen. We follow behind him, Laney fiddling with her hands as Marcus turns around offers her a beer.

"Have you seen Luna?" she asks.

"No, why would I?" His nonchalance makes my stomach lurch. I want to *bite* him. I have no idea where such a feral urge comes from but, oh my Goddess, I want to sink my teeth into him until he screams like the little bitch I know he is.

"Someone took her," I snap. "Do you know where she is?"

"What do you mean *someone took her*?" He sits his beer down on the island bar and jumps to his feet, obviously shocked.

I stumble backwards, surprised by the display. I hadn't expected that reaction.

"Is she okay? Do you know who took her?"

"It wasn't you," I whisper, panic sinking deep into my bones. Some part of me had hoped it was Marcus. He's the evil I know. He would be easy to deal with. Luna would be easier to find.

But now.

I lay a hand on my chest as my heart beats out of control.

"Bug?" Laney whispers, coming around to my side.

"Why would someone kidnap her? Who the fuck is she?" Marcus narrows his eyes on me and I try to breathe through the panic attack that threatens to take over.

"Don't pretend like you don't know who she is," I accuse, barely holding onto the idea that Marcus is involved. "I know you know something."

"I know she's not who you *say* she is. But I honestly have no idea who she is. She's powerful though." He shrugs, taking a seat on the barstool. "But I guess if she's gone . . ."

"If she's gone what?" Laney snaps.

"Babe, I just meant—"

"You really are just after power, aren't you?" Laney's voice is icy cold, a strange contrast to the heat I feel radiating from her body where she stands by my side.

"She's a Celestial," I grind out. "Stop fucking around, Marcus. Where is she?"

Marcus' eyes go wide and in that instant, I know he really didn't know anything. He blinks then takes a swig of his beer, shaking his head. "Holy shit. The Moon? That makes sense, now that you've said it. Damn."

"Why?"

Marcus looks to the side and shrugs. "There's been some talk about a Celestial presence on Earth."

"Oh my Goddess, you *do* know something!" Laney roars. Or is it Juniper who roars? I shrug away the confusion. My mind is clouded by the impending panic attack and I need to focus.

The smell of smoke brings me back into the moment and I lurch forward, patting at Marcus' shoulder.

"Really, babe?" he snarls, glaring at the two of us. "Jealousy doesn't suit you."

"What do you know? Or I'm going to let her charbroil you."

"When I was talking to my parents about your visitor, they weren't as interested in the powerful new witch as they usually would be. They were busy gossiping about a Celestial who was apparently on Earth. The first one in thousands of years. Apparently some dark witches are searching for her."

"Why were you telling your parents about Luna?" I'm not entirely sure why Laney keeps asking him these questions. He's all but admitted the truth to her. I know she wants to believe the best in him, but in this moment, if she can't see him for what he is, then she's blind.

"They want me to make the best match possible," he shrugs. "You know that."

"And I'm not good enough?" Laney's voice is pure fire. Judging by the rising temperature around us, that fire is in danger of escaping her any second. I trust her, she's got excellent control of her element. But all that means is that the fire will go exactly where she wants it to when she finally gives in to it, and I wouldn't want to be Marcus when that happens.

"You're everything I could hope for, Laney." He takes a step toward her but quickly stops when small flames appear on the floor in front of him. "I couldn't not tell my parents about someone as powerful as Luna, though. Babe, you have to understand. To them . . . power is everything."

"To you, power is everything," she shrieks.

"Who are the witches your parents were talking to about the

Celestial?" I ask between their outbursts. Part of me is ecstatic that Laney is finally dumping this idiot but I can't focus on that right now.

"Uh," Marcus stammers, rubbing a hand down the back of his head. "I can't really—" The flames on the expensive flooring grow larger and he swallows. "I don't know. I know there's dark witches living in Waitsfield, but that's all I can say."

The flames extinguish and Laney grabs my hand pulling me back. A large shadow falls over Marcus' face and I twist in her grip to get a better view of Beezlebub landing on his face, wings fully open.

"Fuck! Get it off me!" he yells, swatting at my poor familiar.

Beezlebub chitters away, clinging to the idiot's nose for another second before flying toward me and Laney.

"But we don't know who they are," I remind Laney as she slams open the door.

"I have some spells we can try. I need to leave, Bug, before I burn this fucking house to the ground."

"Yeah, that's probably not the best—"

"Okay then." Her tone leaves no room for argument. I follow her out to the car and open the driver door. As I glance at my sister over the top of the car, the smell of smoke hits me and I panic.

"Laney," I murmur.

"Wait."

As I toss the keys from my left hand to my right hand and back again the smell of smoke grows thicker. The house door slams open and out comes Marcus, hands in his hair as he stares at a spot in the yard.

"Fucking really?!"

Laney snorts and jumps into the passenger seat. I stand on my tiptoes, trying to see far enough to make out what all the fuss is about. In the yard, several patches of grass have been burnt to read: Marcus Welling is a cheat.

With a laugh, I shake my head and slip into the car, quickly starting it. As I back out of the driveway, I glance at Laney. "Couldn't think of anything more inventive?"

"Shut up, Bug." She flips the bird to the property as we leave and I turn off the heater. The heat coming from my pissed off sister is more than enough to keep us warm on our way home.

"What are these spells you want to try?" I ask, changing the subject.

"You knew he was a dick the whole time," she sighs, shaking her head in my peripheral vision. "A scrying spell. If we can't get it to work, Mom might be able to. She's always been great at that."

My fingers drum on the steering wheel as I consider that. Scrying is easy enough. I just really want to find Luna. It's like a weight in my chest I can't swallow or get rid of, and I know the only thing that will make it okay is seeing she's alright.

Chapter 19
Luna

My stomach clenches as I jerk awake to the sound of strangers speaking. My eyes fly open but the darkness remains. Itchy cloth brushes against my nose as my face moves and I realize I'm blindfolded. Annoyance surges inside me. I try to pull my hand forward but it's secured behind my back.

"What are we going to do with her when she wakes up?" a disembodied voice asks from somewhere nearby.

Yes, you should be very worried about what will happen when 'she' wakes up, mortals. Focusing, I summon the magic within me to untie my wrists but nothing happens.

Panic slams into me as I realize I can't access my magic at all.

"We just have to keep her sedated until the solstice. That's when her power will be at its full strength."

"We will be Gods," the first voice replies reverently.

A frustrated growl escapes my throat as I try over and over to access my magic. Nothing. They must have drugged me. Images of Alandra falling to the floor in the smoke-filled bedroom flash across my lids and desperation claws at my chest.

I need to know she's okay. I need to know she wasn't harmed by the gas.

"Someone's awake," a deep voice rumbles close by my ear.

I jerk away from the sound and turn my head, refusing to participate in whatever game this witch is playing.

"Aw, don't be like that. There's no need to be rude. This is simply business, honestly," he purrs. A calloused finger brushes my cheek and a revolted shudder climbs up my spine.

"Do not be so bold as to touch me, witch," I hiss blindly to whatever fool is before me.

"So she speaks."

Pursing my lips, I relax into the uncomfortable chair I'm bound to. Giving them a reaction will only spur them on. I may not know much about this new world the mortals have built for themselves, or the technology they've filled it with, but one thing has remained the same: The cruelty of mortals is unparalleled.

They think the Gods are cruel, but truly, I've never met anything so vicious as a mortal being. Their desperation clings to them like a stink they can't get rid of, no matter how hard they try. They all fight the death that is inevitably theirs. It's pathetic and it's always driven them to unspeakable acts.

Like Orion. An all too familiar feeling of dread passes through me. When Orion was on the brink of death, when he knew he was never going to make it home, his consciousness sought out the rest of the Celestials. His pain poured into each of us, filling us with the horror of what was happening to him. I can see it now as clearly as I could see it then.

It felt like starlight poured from my own mouth as I channeled his death. My eyes wept tears but the burning sensation of energy streaming from them wouldn't stop.

I shake my head, dismissing the memory. If that is my fate, there's nothing I can do about it. But I won't give up so easily. I'll fight to the end.

"We thank you for your sacrifice, Moon Spirit."

Ah, so they know who I am.

"I do not agree to be your sacrifice nor do I enter into any contract with your coven. I wish to be freed, let go, to continue my existence of my own free will as ordained by the Great Goddess upon my creation. I refute any attempt to harness my power, I rebuke any attempt on my body. I am not yours, witch." The words are poison in my mouth and I can't stop speaking until they're all out.

The soft chuckle in the dark send ice through my veins.

"We do not need your permission, Celestial. But your objections are noted."

Footsteps echo throughout the room around me as the witch walks away. Defeated, I focus on all the magic around me. At least I can still sense them.

At least twenty flames flicker with varying intensities all around me. Some seem to be on top of me, which tells me I must be underground. My nostrils flare as I scent the air around me and accept the idea I'm underground. Everything smells damp and earthy.

Alandra, I plead silently with the universe. *Where are you?*

But, of course, there's no reply. My love doesn't have the type of magic necessary to hear my plea. The magic she does have is locked so far away inside her, even she doesn't see her true worth.

Her true power.

I should have explained it to her when I had the chance. If I had, maybe I wouldn't be in the predicament I am now. I blow out a huff. The spell trapping me in this realm ends on the solstice. If I can make it until my powers are returned, I can flee before any permanent harm is done.

Please, Great Mother, help me through this ordeal. I've never asked for anything. I have never once called upon you or disturbed your eternal sleep. I would never dare under normal circumstances. Help me, your creations plan to end me.

I focus all of my mental strength on sending the prayer out into the universe, hoping the Great Goddess will hear my plea and take mercy. A quick, stinging pain assaults my neck and my hold on the waking world slips away once again.

Chapter 20
Alandra

We stare into the bowl of scrying water, watching the ripples twist and turn directions as they try to locate Luna. We've been at this for over an hour. Laney had even gone as far as to pour out the bowl and start completely from scratch.

So far, we've gotten absolutely nowhere, despite our best efforts. Beezlebub lands on the edge of the bowl, chittering away at the water and I shake my head. Somewhere nearby Juniper growls, mirroring the grunts of frustration coming from my sister.

"I don't understand!" Laney snarls as she pushes the bowl away. The water laps at the edge and Beezlebub lifts his front leg, avoiding the wet fiasco, but just barely.

"They have to be blocking her location somehow," I sigh. "Would you know how to do something like that?"

"Block my location?" Laney scrunches her nose up. "Yes. I've done it before. But the way I'm scrying for her, it shouldn't matter. They must have layers of protection around wherever they're holding or. Or—"

I shake my head, swallowing hard. "No, no 'or'."

"Bug, we need to prepare ourselves for the fact that she might already be gone." Laney lays a hand on my shoulder and I shrug away from her, taking a deep breath.

"I'd know if she were dead."

"How?"

"I—I can't explain it," I choke out, holding a hand to my heart. "I feel her inside me, sometimes. It's like a piece of her is with me."

"Oh fuck," Laney whispers, her eyes going wide. "Did you bind yourself to her?"

"What? No! Of course not," I mumble, wiping at the tears gathering in my eyes. "There's just something . . . there. I don't know how to explain it."

"It sounds like you're bound. But you can't do that accidentally," Laney admits, chewing her lower lip. "You love her, don't you?"

I blink owlishly at her, my heartbeat slowing along with everything around me. Do I love her? Beezlebub's soft legs and silken wings slide against my neck as he crawls under my hair to hide or show his support—who knows which, honestly—and I nod. I do.

I know I shouldn't. I know there's absolutely no way this ends well for me. But something inside me loves Luna for all the strange, wonderful things that she is. Her graceful weird complements my awkward strange.

"I think I do," I mumble quietly.

"Awe, Bug," Laney sighs, shoving a hand in her hair. "I told you not to get attached to her!"

"Well, it wasn't exactly a part of my master plan, Laney," I snarl. Juniper pads over between us and bares her teeth. Her large tongue curls over the sharp edges and I swear her eyes narrow. She's never liked when anyone raises their voice to Laney.

"Yeah, I'm sure," she sighs, pinching the bridge of her nose. "Okay. That's a problem for a different day. Right now, we need to find your girlfriend and keep her from being sacrificed. No big deal."

"I mean, there's always a chance that she isn't being sacrificed?" My voice sounds hopeful, even to me, and Laney just dead-pans before flipping through a book for a new spell to try.

"Yeah, I know," I sigh. My phone buzzes in my pocket, a long continuous vibration which means someone is calling. My eyebrows scrunch down as I pull it out and press the green answer key.

"Mom?" I ask, confused.

"Sweetie, what time are you two coming over?"

I look to Laney, a question on my face. "I don't think we were planning on coming over? Mom, what is this—"

"Of course not, you're over there trying to fix this all by yourselves because you don't trust your own mother. Goddess. Just come over here, now please." She ends the call with a sniff and my hand drops, staring down at the screen.

"What the hell was that about?"

"I have no idea. I think she knows?" The hairs on the back of my neck prickle and I swat at the creepy sensation. "Do you think we have a ghost in here?"

"No." Laney shakes her head, but the way her eyes widen when she glances around the room makes me wonder if she believes her own lie.

Mom takes her time pouring the tea. My foot bounces under the table nervously as she inclines her head toward yet another invisible guest and speaks quietly.

"It's bizarre," I sigh.

"You'd think after growing up with her, you'd be used to it," Laney laughs. Her eyes dart around the room, even as she tosses me a carefree smile. It unnerves her too, she just doesn't want to hurt Mom's feelings.

"Girls," Mom interrupts, setting a cup of tea down in front of each of us. "Tell me what's been going on, please. I try so hard not to interfere, but the things I'm hearing—" She shakes her head and takes a seat across the table, folding her hands on the table as she waits for one of us to explain.

Laney and I exchange worried glances but finally, I shrug. Luna has already been kidnapped. What's the harm in telling Mom? Besides, I think she already knows some of it. *Damn ghosts.*

"Someone took Luna," I explain carefully. "She was kidnapped from our house and we're trying to find her."

"Why would someone do that?" Mom asks, much too calmly.

I narrow my eyes on her and cross my arms over my chest. "I have a feeling you already know, don't you?"

"That you summoned, slept with, and *lost* The Moon?" Mom rolls her eyes heavenward as she stirs her own cup of tea. "Yes, I've been made aware."

"Why didn't you say anything? When did you know?" My hand slams down on the table, punctuating my words with a hollow sounding smack.

"I was told during dinner," Mom admits quietly, meeting my eyes. "You really summoned Luna from her realm? How?" She looked impressed but sad.

"I fucked up the blessing, somehow. Mom, do you know where she is?" My hand waves around vaguely to the rest of the room, to the spirits I know must be there even though I can't see them. "Have they seen her?" I really should be more concerned with the fact that my mom kept this information to herself instead of confronting me. What else does she know? What else has she kept to herself over the years?

It's disconcerting.

"Where's Dad?" Laney asks suddenly, looking around. He takes Yule off, every year. As an insurance agent, he can work from home when necessary. But his car wasn't here when we pulled up either . . .

"I'm not sure," Mom whispers, a frown pulling her lips down. Her head cocks to the side and her eyes narrow before she pulls out her cellphone. Before any of us can speak, the phone is on speaker, ringing as she calls Dad.

"Audrey?"

"Sterlen, where are you, hun? The girls are here." Mom meets my eyes across the table and I arch an eyebrow.

"I'm uh—" the sound of muffled voices echoes in the background. "I'm helping some friends with solstice preparations. What's going on? Are the girls okay?"

"They seem alright," Mom answers slowly.

"Not sick?"

"Why would they be sick, Sterlen?" Mom asks, her voice cracking like a whip.

I shake my head, my heart rate speeding up.

"I was just worried is all. The girls never just pop over, I figured something must be wrong."

"Sterlen, hun, who are you helping for the solstice?" Mom's eyes narrow further, a bright red flush creeping up her neck to her cheeks.

"The Prathers, why, love?" Dad whispers something to someone in the background I can't quite make out. "Look, I have to go, Audrey. Tell the girls I love them, I'll see you all later tonight."

The call ends and I look nervously from Mom, who is fuming, to Laney, whose mouth is gaping. I'm not sure what to accuse Dad of at this point. Is he fucking around on Mom again? Or is this as bad as it sounds? He even asked if I was sick . . .

"Mom, what's going on?" I ask, leaning forward, my elbows bracing heavily on the table.

"I—I don't know. They've been telling me things for a while, things I didn't want to believe." A tear rolls down Mom's cheek and she shakes her head, wiping at the salty path in her makeup. "Spirits aren't infallible, you know. They're just what's left of people. And some people are bad, and some people are good . . . I'd hoped this was just their version of idle gossip."

"You hoped *what* was their version of idle gossip?" Laney asks, mirroring my own body language. We're literally on the edge of our seats, trying to get to the bottom of this when mom looks away, to something we can't see.

"Your father comes from a line of dark witches," she finally whispers.

"*What?!*" I screech, standing so fast, my chair slams back into the wall behind me.

"Alandra, sit down."

"Holy fuck," Laney whispers, covering her mouth with her hand. "How long have you known?"

"A spirit told me when I met him during college. I asked him about it and he told me the truth. He came from a family that practiced on the darker side, blood magic, southern hoodoo, you know the type," she sighs, shaking her head. "But he never wanted anything to do with all that. I couldn't blame him for his family. You can't *choose* who brings you into this world, girls. So, we moved past it. We fell in love." She smiles sadly at the two of us. "We started a family."

"Mom," I whisper, my voice shaking with rage. "Only dark witches would have taken Luna. You know what they did to Orion. Are those the witches Dad comes from?" My head hurts. I think I might actually have a Gods damned aneurysm after all this. What is wrong with the women in my family that they attract these assholes?

Is my Dad an asshole? He has definitely cheated on my mom before, so 'asshole' is probably fitting. But is he evil? I groan internally as my mind tries to sort the details out.

Did he take Luna?

"Yes. Your father's family has been a part of The Order for generations. It's why you girls have never met them. I didn't want you influenced by the wrong kind of magic."

"Oh my Goddess," I whisper, shaking my head. "He took Luna. Or he told someone who took her. Mom, where is he?"

"Who are the Prathers?" Laney asks, rubbing her temples. At least I'm not the only one with a headache from all of this.

"The Prathers were banished from Waitsfield when I was a child. They live near the state park. They were banished for practicing dark magic. This came out during the Enlightenment, when witches across the world were revealing themselves to humans, and the Waitsfield Coven didn't want to be tied to their . . . ideals." Mom grimaces, casting a wayward glance at her phone. "I don't know where they live, exactly, but I can find your father. If you think——"

"Do it. Now." My teeth grind together as I push the words out. It takes everything in me not to scream. My dad had made such a scene in front of Luna and he's tied to these awful people?

He may have actually taken her? My *father* may have drugged me, put me in danger, and taken a woman from my bed in the middle of the night? What kind of Shakespearian drama am I living in?

"Bug," Laney whispers, reaching out to touch my arm. I dodge her touch and shake my head. I don't want to be consoled right now. We've already done that somewhere along this emotional rollercoaster.

I don't want to pretend everything is going to be okay. I don't want platitudes. I want to be angry. I want that rage to seep into my very bones and fuel me. I don't have as much magic to rely on as my sister or my mother. I don't have dead spies who can tell me what my enemies are up to from across town. I only have this rage.

And no one is going to take that from me right now.

"He is where he said he is," Mom finally says, her eyes fluttering open. "Somewhere in Mt. Mansfield State Park, I think. Girls, I don't want to believe your father could have done this—" She takes a deep breath and then meets each of our eyes before continuing. "But the things the spirits have been telling me . . . I think maybe he isn't the man I thought he was. I'm so sorry, lovies." A single tear slides down her cheek and Laney leans over the table, consoling her.

The words mumbled between them are probably sweet. It's probably heartwarming. But I'm not interested. Beezlebub chitters angrily near my ear. "Yeah, me too, boy," I murmur, nuzzling my cheek down against his fuzzy face. He's just as pissed as I am.

"Alandra," Mom says and my head snaps in her direction.

"Yes?"

"Can you forgive me?"

"You didn't take her, Mom," I sigh. "I'm not mad at you. I just want her back. And Dad better hope we're wrong and he's not involved in this. Because *that*, I won't be able to forgive."

Mom nods, sniffling as she pushes her chair away from her table. "If he's with a coven, we'll need some things to protect ourselves. Come on."

Laney and I follow mom out of the kitchen and down the hall toward the altar room. My parents are more traditional that me and my sister. Where we practice in the living room, right by the window, they practice in a room solely dedicated to magic.

As we enter the room, mom whispers, *"Ad lucium."* Several candles flicker to life as the magic in the house rolls across my skin like a warm breeze. I glance around the room and an unkind nostalgia worms its way into my heart. This room holds many memories and many mixed emotions.

An old pentagram which has been painted and repainted is still displayed on the floor draws my eye and a shudder rocks my body. I'd sat in that fucking circle more times than I could count as my parents tried to summon my 'missing magic'. The spells they tried were sometimes horrendous, bordering on child abuse by today's standards.

Bordering might be pushing it. It probably *was* child abuse by today's standards, but painting my parents in that light is hard for me to swallow. Even now.

"Alandra," Mom calls out over her shoulder and I step carefully around the painted edges of the circle until I meet her by an old trunk. "Take these."

"What are they?" I examine the first little bag and sniff it suspiciously.

"Defensive hex bags. I've used them in the past—"

"Mom, when would you need to use something like those?" Laney asks, crossing her arms once again.

"Things weren't always so peaceful in Waitsfield, girls," Mom huffs, shaking her head. "Take them, Alandra. My affinity is passive so I learned how to defend myself a long time ago. Throw these and say *stupefaciunt* and you'll stun whoever it hits. It's not perfect, but it's helpful for witches like us."

My eyes blink repeatedly. I look from my mother to the tiny bag in my hand and then begin stuffing them in my pockets. I can't believe she's never mentioned something like this before. I could think of plenty of occasions where this kind of magic would have come in handy.

"Like us," I laugh, as the last part of her sentence finally resonates inside me. "I'm nothing like you."

Mom opens her mouth to speak but I just grab a few more hex bags and turn to leave. Laney's muffled voice sounds behind me as I make my way down the hall. I could go my entire life never being in that room again. And I plan on it.

Chapter 21

Alandra

I turn right onto the narrow highway that leads toward Mt. Mansfield State Park, side-eying my mom where she leans against the window. All the rage swirling in my own stomach can't compare to whatever she's feeling.

My dad is an idiot. He's betrayed her before, despite being bound, but this is a new level of hurt for our entire family. How could he hide something like this from us? My entire life has been spent thinking I'm not good enough and he's a dark witch? How is that fair?

"Will you stay with him?" I ask quietly, making it a point to keep my eyes forward, focused on the road.

"I don't know," she sighs. "I never thought I'd have to make a decision like this. Neither of you are bound yet, so you don't understand what it feels like. A piece of your dad's magic lives inside me, and a piece of mine is inside him."

"But he's cheated on you, how is it possible if you're—"

"Laney, stop," Mom sniffs. "People can make mistakes even when they're connected. It's just rare and even more of a blow when it does happen." Mom's voice tugs at a sadness inside me. I'm not bound to Luna, but I could be. I'd agree to it in a heartbeat. I've never felt this strongly this fast for anyone ever.

"I'm sorry, Mom." The GPS dings, updating the estimated time of arrival as we make our way toward Mansfield. "What if she's already dead?" I ask in a small, defeated voice.

"You said yourself you'd feel it if she were."

"Your father is a smart man, despite whatever else he may be. He'll know that her power is the fullest at the height of the solstice. He'll wait until then." Mom rubs a hand down my arm and I smile weakly, refusing to look in her direction.

My eyes flick to Laney's in the rearview mirror and the look of panic across her face makes me groan.

"What is it?"

"Luna is trapped here until the solstice." Her face goes white as she whispers the words. "It might be close."

"I can't believe Dad would do this," I sputter, unable to wrap my mind around my father being this evil, shrouded figure. "She's a woman. He'd hurt a woman?"

"I'm not entirely sure who he is anymore, Alandra..."

"To them, she's not a person. She's an ingredient to a spell, a sacrificial lamb who has to be slaughtered," Laney adds, unhelpfully. "If they knew her, if they valued her as a person, they wouldn't be able to go through with the spellwork. Compartmentalization. It's a thing, unfortunately."

"You'd still stay with him if he killed her?" I ask Mom quietly. Laney goes silent. You could cut the tension with a knife as my mother squirms in her seat.

"You can't be closer than being bound," she finally whispers. "I don't know if I can leave him after being bound for so long. But something has to be done. Something has to change."

I shake my head, unsure of what that means. It sounds like a political non-answer to me, but then again Audrey Michaels is better at those than anybody. She heads most of the charities and foundations in Waitsfield and organizes things on a national level when asked to by the council.

But it's still a non-answer. My teeth dig into the side of my cheek as I push down on the accelerator. Every second counts right now. I don't know what the consequences for our world would be if something were to happen to her. All I know is this is my fucked up family's fault, I need to stop it, and the consequences for *me* would be irreparable.

In the back seat, Laney unclicks her seatbelt and leans up over the center console to turn the radio dial. It takes a few tries and a few talk-shows until she finds what she's looking for, but eventually a soft rock song fills the car and she leans back once again.

"I'm sorry, girls," Mom whispers.

"We know, Mom." Laney blows out a heavy sigh before I hear the tell-tale click of her seatbelt being fastened again.

"I just need to get her back."

"Oh, honey," Mom murmurs softly, brushing her hand over my hair. "I know. We'll get her."

Chapter 22
Alandra

The tires fight for something to grasp as I pull into a snow-covered parking lot. It hasn't been salted or plowed it what looks like forever. My eyes drift past the two cars in the corner of the lot and land on the red two-seater Dad bought a few years ago.

The pentagram necklace hanging from the rearview mirror glints in the setting sun and my stomach turns over on itself. He really is here. Is she? I'm torn between hoping she's here so I can get her back and praying my Dad isn't involved in all of this. Denial only goes so far, but I guess no one wants to admit their parents are monsters.

I put the car in park and stare at the edge of the woods. The sun is setting. The solstice is tomorrow. My fingers drum rhythmically against the steering wheel as both Mom and Laney unclick their seat belts.

"This is . . . problematic," Mom points out.

"Why?"

Laney takes a deep breath and leans up against the center console to explain. "If there's a coven of dark witches in that forest, then it's probably attuned to them. That means the Earth here won't lend us any help and our magic might be weakened. Worst case scenario? The woods actually turn against us."

"Is that a thing that can happen?"

"It's rare," Mom mumbles, looking through her purse for something.

I take a deep breath and remember the words Mom spoke at the house. If anyone jumps out at me, I'm just going to throw the hex bag first and ask questions later. It seems fair enough at this point, honestly.

The last bit of fading sunlight reflects off the parked cars and I take a deep breath. The air is so fresh up here, nothing but the heady scent of pine and fir trees and the bitter snap of snow. The forest looks as uninviting as one place could possibly be. Shadows dance just inside the tree line and a shiver zips up my spine. Is there someone there?

"Come on," Laney growls, marching across the parking lot toward the trees. "The longer we wait, the darker it gets, the closer the solstice is. We only have until tomorrow, Bug. Let's go."

I steel my spine, pulling one of the hex bags out of my pocket—just in case—and follow my sister toward the creepy looking forest. A soft chittering grabs my attention the second before Beezlebub flies around my head and charges into the hooded part of my jacket. He clings to the material, the soft, fuzzy part of his body rubbing against my cheek with every step I take. Snow crunches under my boots as we draw closer to the edge of the woods.

"What are we doing?" I mumble under my breath.

"Saving your girlfriend," Laney sighs, pushing past me as she takes the first step into the woods. A fireball hovers above her left palm, lighting up the area around us as trudge through the underbrush and tall trees.

"I want to hear more about that," Mom adds, picking her way carefully around a fallen log. "When this is over."

I cringe, trying to imagine *that* conversation. I don't even know what Luna thinks or wants. She lives in a different plane of existence. I broke up with Jess because she moved across the country. If I couldn't handle that sort of long-distance relationship, how could I possibly date the fucking Moon?

And what's to say Luna was even interested in pursuing whatever this is between us? There's definitely something here, I know that for certain. The way she looked at me when we made love was different. The way she kissed me, worked me up into a ball of need and then rolled away, offering only snuggles . . . everything she did felt different to me, somehow.

Snap!

My feet freeze in place, my fingers clutching the hex bag as we scan the area around us. No one speaks, just standing there waiting for whatever is to come. An owl hoots in the tree above us and I let out a nervous chuckle.

"Goddess," Mom sighs, moving ahead of us. "We're close. Next time it could actually be something."

As I duck under barren branches and crash through the snow-packed leaf litter, my stomach begins to twist and roll once again. Every shadow we pass has my heart slamming to a stop, just waiting for an attack to come.

"Fucking hell," I mutter, and collide firmly against Mom's back. I bounce off her and right myself, ignoring the angry chitters from Beezlbub. A quiet growl in the woods beside us has me jumping into a defensive stance, hex bag at the ready until Laney lays a hand on my arm.

"It's just Juniper, calm down. We're here." She nods in the direction Mom is facing and I look past her at the small clearing. A large, very abandoned looking house looms against the wooded backdrop. Every horror movie I've ever watched has taught me you run away from houses like this one, not toward them. But here we are.

"He's in there," Mom whispers quietly.

I grab her hand and squeeze, surveying the house once again before stepping out into the clearing. Laney hisses in a breath and follows me with Mom on her heels. As we get to the bottom of the stairs, I swallow hard.

"Well, it definitely looks like an evil lair." Most of the windows are boarded up. Parts of the porch railing are missing, some even hang down the side. Pieces of wood and a few empty beer bottles litter the ground at the bottom of the stairs. The door has a crack in it, but no light filters out into the dark with us.

"Yup. Let's go into the creepy house," Laney mutters, taking the steps one at a time. She sounds confident, but the tiny fireball in her hand tells me she's nervous. I don't blame her. My fingers cling to the hex bag, ready to throw it at the first sign of trouble.

Mom is standing so close behind me, I can *feel* her there. It's not helping the overall creepy aesthetic. As Laney takes the first, creaky step onto the dilapidated porch, the front door flies open. Wood splinters fly out as a black mass of shadow swarms onto the porch.

"Shit, there's a caster!" Laney snarls, ducking low before I lose sight of her completely. Casting is a devious affinity. Casters can manifest shadow on command, in all of its forms. A low snarl pricks my ears through the absolute darkness. Two bright red eyes meet mine and I gulp, my fingers digging into the small canvas pouch as I prepare to stand my ground.

It's just a manifestation, I tell myself. *It's not actually a monster. It's a trick.* But the panic prancing through my chest doesn't care about logic. The shapeless mass prowls closer and I throw the hex bag. It falls through the illusion, sinking quickly until it finally strikes something solid.

"*Stupefaciunt!*" I shout.

Slowly, the shadows engulfing us dissipate. On the porch lays a man, not much older than me. A mask hangs from the side of his head, covering half of his face. His eyes, or at least the one eye I can see clearly, are shut, his mouth hanging open like someone in a very deep sleep.

"Wow," I gasp, surveying the damage. Those bags really do pack a punch.

"Get off of me!" Laney's screams pierce my ears and I turn just in time to see her head disappear under a piece of fabric. As soon as she's covered, she slumps against the two men holding her. The smell of smoke and burning fabric wafts from their singed clothes. Small rings of fire burn into the porch around them, but as Laney is dragged away, the fires smolder to nothing but smoke.

"Let her go!" I snap, pulling another hexbag from my pocket.

"Alandra!" Mom calls out. My head snaps in her direction to find a bag being shoved over her head as well. I swallow, looking between the people grabbing my mother and the people dragging Laney through the door. Taking a step back, I try to decide what to do. A snarl under the porch catches my attention. *Juniper.* A harsh growl comes next, and my heart pounds as I realize Juniper is in her own fight with some familiar.

My back hits something hard, yet soft and I turn slowly to face whoever I've just run into. My eyes meet the tall, wide shouldered man's masked face only a second before he grabs my wrist and rips the hexbag from my grasp.

"You're hurting me!" I cry out as the bones in my hand and wrist grind together, threatening to crack under the pressure. I don't know why I thought he'd care.

Darkness surrounds me. A foul scent assaults my nostrils before my eyes begin to sag shut. My knees buckle and a firm hand grabs my upper arm. Beezlebub chitters hopelessly into my ear as the world fades away.

A POUNDING PAIN PULLS ME OUT OF UNCONSCIOUSNESS. MY HEAD FEELS like someone's been playing the drums on it. Or kickball with it. I groan, instinctively pulling my hand up to rub my temples but it catches on something. Jerking my hand one more time, I let out a soft growl of frustration as I realize my hands are bound behind my back.

What the fuck?

Memories of what happened on the porch flood my mind, piece by jagged piece, like an onslaught of broken glass. Everything hurts, even remembering.

"You weren't supposed to hurt them!" a familiar voice whisper-screams. Even the small noise is too much right now. What is with these people and migraine-inducing magic? There were so many better options out there. Like not being evil cunts. "You were just supposed to scare them off! Now, what the hell am I supposed to do?"

To his credit, at least Dad seemed concerned about our safety.

"It's not going to matter, soon, Michaels. You'll be a God when then is through. You can piece your little family back together then." This voice sounded like they had gravel in their throat. Images of an old man, stooped over his cane pass across the back of my lids.

"Yes, Sterlen," Mom snarls from somewhere nearby. "Tell me how you plan to piece your family back together. Tell us all how, precisely, you think you can fix this massive mess you've made."

"Quiet, Audrey," Dad hisses. Footsteps falling on a hard floor echo throughout whatever room we're in.

"Oh, are you going to gag me, too? Is that what you've come to, Sterlen? You used to be such a good man," she sniffles. It's obvious she's been crying. *Poor Mom.*

Soft chittering catches my attention as a light weight lands on my forehead. *Beezlebub.* His tiny legs tickle as he pushes at the dark material covering my eyes.

"Good job, B," I whisper as the first sliver of light peeks through the loosened blindfold. A fire smolders in the middle of the room. The glow of the flames taunt me behind the dark piece of fabric. Beezlebub pushes at it, working it down slowly as my parents continue arguing.

"I was raised for this opportunity!" My father snaps. "I've tried my best to be a good husband, a good father. I fall short, sometimes, but I think I'm a decent man. Don't hate me for something I was born to do."

"You were born to murder an innocent woman?" I hiss as the blindfold finally falls down my face. Beezlebub skitters back along my neck, hiding in my hair.

"Alandra," Dad sighs, turning toward me. The cloak billows around him as he turns and I can't help but snort. He looks like something from a bad straight-to-TV-movie. His mask is pushed up into his hairline, his frustrated face visible as he addresses me. "She's not a witch, she's not even human."

"She's a fucking Celestial!" I snap.

"Lower your voice. Your sister is sleeping."

My eyes dart to the left and fall on Laney, her head dropped forward with a blindfold tied around her eyes. Luna sits on the other side of her, her white hair and pale skin shining softly in the dimly lit room. If there was any doubt what she was, the glow would remove it. Her head head snaps in my direction, her mouth parting, but she says nothing.

"Sleeping, huh? She looks like she's drugged, to me. Scared your little girl will wake up and burn Daddy's evil lair to the ground?"

"That's enough!" He marches toward me and I cringe. At this point, I wouldn't be surprised if he struck me. Like Mom said, he's a completely different person.

"You leave her alone!" she growls from her chair. For all her struggling, the thing only rocks against the concrete floor, barely moving at all. Her head whips from side to side, trying to shake the blindfold loose as she panics. It's a bizarre experience, watching my mother fear for my well being at the hands of my father.

"Listen to your wife, *Sterlen*," Luna snarls. I know that she can't see him through the blindfold but I swear it looks like she's staring directly at him. My heart skips a beat; hearing her voice let's me know she's actually alright. Maybe we will make it through this.

"And I thought I told you to let me handle my own daughter?" he snaps.

He's never been the best Dad. He's always been too hard on me, always put Laney above me—they've both done that—but he's never been abusive physically. Mentally? Yep. Emotionally? Absolutely. The man oozes toxicity. But he'd never laid a hand on me, or anyone else that I'd ever seen.

Dad bends down, interrupting my thoughts, his eyes inches away from mine. "I'm sorry, it wasn't supposed to be like this," he whispers, shoving a hand in his hair. "I never wanted any of this."

My heart pangs for him. He actually sounds upset. "It's not too late to fix it, Dad. Let us go. Let *her* go. We'll get through this together."

Dad shakes his head, blowing out a heavy sigh as he stands back to his full height. "One day you'll understand." With that, he walks away, leaving us alone in the room with only a fire and the soft sounds of Laney's sleepy breathing to keep us company.

"Are you okay?" Mom asks when the footsteps finally stop echoing.

"I'm alright, Mom," I assure her. At least physically.

Chapter 23
Luna

Something soft lands on my forehead and I freeze for a moment. Instantly, reassuring magic washes over me and I sigh softly. "Beezlebub."

He chitters graciously at the acknowledgement, trying to push my blindfold down as Alandra and her Mother speak quietly to one another.

"I don't understand why he'd do this," Alandra sniffs.

"I'm sorry your father turned out to be this . . . person." Audrey sounds distant, like all of her emotions have abandoned her to the despair that is this underground hell. And it's definitely underground.

Before Beezlebub can finish pushing the blindfold down, I'm once again lost in the damp, earthy smell of this place. The smoke from the fire covers some of the scent, but it's still there. Deep, damp soil. We're in a basement somewhere.

"Luna, are you alright?" Alandra asks, her voice timid.

I turn toward the sound and smile, nodding as the blindfold finally slips down to my neck. Her hair is mussed, puffed oddly by the blindfold around her neck. Her blue eyes shimmer with emotions and I wish I could go to her, caress her cheek and tell her everything will be alright.

On instinct, I tug at my hands and a snarl rips from my throat as frustration settles over me. My magic is still locked away where I can't reach it. "I can't help us," I tell her. "They've bound me somehow."

"Bound you?" Alandra asks, her eyebrows cinching down with

worry. Beezlebub flits away from me toward Audrey and begins working on her blindfold next.

"They've muted her powers. There's spells for it, though I'm shocked they'd work on someone like her."

"Their order would know. How else would they have been able to contain Orion?" I sigh, my head hanging low.

"It's going to be okay," Alandra rushes out. "We will figure this out, I promise. I'm sorry. This is all my fault." My head snaps up in time to see a tear slip down her cheek and I shake my head.

"Don't say that."

"It's true. If I could do one damn spell right, you wouldn't even be here. You'd still be safe in your home."

"But—"

"I'm so sorry," she whispers, gazing past me, to the fire at the other side of the room.

"Love, if you only knew how much joy knowing you has been. Even if they end me, my existence has been more full since you summoned me than it has been since my creation."

Alandra's gaze slams into mine, fresh tears brewing in the corners. Her bottom lip trembles as she blinks the tears away, unable to wipe her face. I hate to see her this way, tied to a chair. This moment shouldn't be sullied by the depravities of these dark witches. If I could give her a perfect moment, I would.

"Wow," Audrey murmurs as her blindfold slips free. Beezlebub quickly moves back to Alandra and nuzzles into her neck. I wish I could do the same, but he will have to cuddle her enough for the both of us.

"Yes?" I ask, focusing on Audrey. She seems disgusted by the situation, by her husband. At least there's some sense of loyalty among women, still, even if witches can't be trusted.

"We have to get you out of here," she mumbles, glancing around the room for the first time. "There has to be something we can use."

"Unfortunately, your husband is smart. There's nothing nearby that would help us and I can't access my magic." I don't want to say we're doomed, because it's not fair to Alandra. It's also not true. I'm doomed. Alandra, Laney, and Audrey are probably safe. I doubt Sterlen would actually harm them. He wants my power, that's all.

That's all.

"I love you," Alandra whispers quietly, so low that I might have missed it if it wasn't for the quiet room we're locked away in. "I know that's weird and awful and my fault and you don't owe me anything. But I do. I love you. I'm sorry. I just want you to know that, in case—"

"I love you too, Little Witch," I chuckle with a soft smile. Her entire face lights up as the words sink in.

"That's . . . adorable. But we need to wake Laney up, somehow. If either of us can get us out of her, it's her. Her fire is a force to be reckoned with."

I raise an eyebrow at Audrey even as Alandra rolls her eyes. Does this woman honestly think her daughter is more powerful than me? But maybe she's right. It couldn't hurt to have one more head in the game, at least. I push my ego aside and close my eyes. "I can try to reach her in her dreamscape," I offer.

"That would be wonderful," Audrey drawls out slowly.

"Wait, you can dreamwalk?" Alandra gasps and I know she's just had a fun little realization.

My mouth twitches up into a smile as the world fades around me. The transition is slow and rocky compared to the smooth flow I'm used to.

Instead of a curtain of fog, I'm met with static. I can't be sure if its because of what they've done to my powers or what they've done to Laney, but the dreamscape is torn and tattered around the edges, giving way to the reality just on the other side.

"Laney?" I call out in the void, searching for her consciousness. The sound of static sets my teeth on edge as I move through the strange substance coating this plane.

Magic clings to my skin like sticky sap as I try to move forward. Laney's voice rings out from a distance, calling for help. Struggling through the restricting goop trying to freeze me in place, I move toward her. She's just a shadow in the distance, but I can see her.

"Laney!" I try again, louder this time.

"Hello?" she replies. The words echo off walls that don't exist just before a

solid sheet of static separates us.

I push at the barrier, sweat breaking out on my forehead as I try to reach the woman on the other side, but it's no use. As I look down at my feet, I see the magic winding its way up my legs.

"I'm sorry," I murmur. "I can't get to you." I want to help, but if I stay any longer, the magic might lock me away in here as well, and that helps no one. I slam my fist against the static barrier one last time before I open my eyes.

My head swims with the sedation magic. I wonder for a moment if they gave her the same thing as me and it's just affecting her differently because she's a mortal.

"I'm sorry," I stutter finally. "I couldn't reach her. The magic is clouding her mind."

Alandra and Audrey nod slowly, both of them glancing to the snoozing Laney. My heart aches for her. I wish I could have brought her out of the dream with me, she sounded so distressed.

"We have to get out of here," Alandra whimpers, her eyes never leaving her sister. Something stirs in my chest, a warm pressure I'm unaccustomed to.

What is happening to me?

Alandra's eyes snap to mine, a question on her face. Her eyebrow quirks slightly and I tip my head to the side. "Do you feel that?" she asks.

"Feel what?"

"Oh no," Audrey groans, drawing our attention to her. "Describe it."

"Like a heavy, warm weight in my chest, pulling me toward Luna." Beside Alandra, Beezlebub chitters happily.

"Like a warmth spreading throughout me, leading to her," I add, my mouth falling open as soon as the words leave my lips. *We're bonding.*

"You bound my daughter without her consent?" Audrey snaps, her eyes narrowing in my direction.

"Not intentionally, I assure you," I groan.

"We're bound?" Alandra's voice is quiet, almost hopeful.

"It sounds like it," her mother answers impatiently. "For fuck sakes, someone figure out how to wake Laney so we can get out of here."

Chapter 24
Alandra

My eyes blink open and I realize I must have dozed off at some point. That or they drugged us again. A quick glance around the dimly lit room reveals that the fire has burned low, as if it was left unattended for a while. Mom's head rolls against her shoulder and I sigh as I look to my left. I can barely make out Laney, thanks to Luna's soft glow. She's still unconscious.

Luna stares at me with wide, frightened eyes. My heart begins to pound as I try to figure out what has her so afraid.

"No," someone hisses in the distance. My eyes strain to see past the glowing embers of what used to be a fire. Two hooded shadows square off by a door—the exit, maybe? "They're not to be touched."

As recognition slams into me and I realize it's Dad speaking, all my internal warning bells go off. "Laney, wake up," I hiss quietly.

Laney doesn't stir but Mom lifts her head, groaning groggily. "What is it? What's ha—"

"Their familiars have been wreaking havoc since they showed up here, that damn cat has injured two of our people, Michaels." The new voice is louder and much angrier than my father. My eyes squint, trying to make out what's happening.

"I won't let you hurt my family. That's where I draw the line," Dad snarls. The space between them closes and the sounds of a scuffle echo throughout the room.

"Oh Goddess," Mom whispers. "Sterlen!" Fear coats her voice as she begins pulling at the rope bindings. Something soft crawls across my wrist and my heart stutters to a stop until I hear soft mewling noises. I'm not entirely sure what B is up to back there, but I can only pray it's helpful.

"Stop!" Dad snarls. Something slams into the wall but I can't make out what, then the sound of metal clambering to the floor rings out.

"I've had it with you, Michaels," the man says. The man sounds calm, much too calm for someone being pinned against a wall by telekinesis. Luna shakes her head, struggling against the ropes that bind her, but there's nothing she can do.

There's nothing any of us can do.

Dad lets out a sick sounding grunt and the man stumbles away from the wall as he falls to the floor. The lowlight from the fire glints off something protruding from Dad's stomach.

He stabbed him.

He fucking stabbed him.

"Dad!" I scream, struggling to get out of my chair. The legs rock back and forth, threatening to tilt. Beezlebub chitters angrily behind me and I realize what he's up to. He's chewing through the rope. It's slow going, but he's trying. I close my eyes and do something I haven't done in a very long time.

Great Goddess, Mother of All, please protect him. Please protect us. I know he's turned his back on you, I know I'm not the kind of witch you'd favor or even pay attention to, but we need your help. Luna is with us. Please, please Goddess don't let them hurt her. Please protect us.

So mote it be.

My eyes snap open again as the man bends down and pulls the knife from Dad's abdomen. He wipes the blade on my father's cloak and then takes a few steps toward us. As he gets closer, I can see the claw marks on his face. Juniper must have had a go at him, if those angry red lines shredding his cheek are anything to go by.

"Stay away from my family!" Mom snaps, her chest rising and falling with her panic.

The witch turns his attention toward her and narrows his eyes. "Wait your turn, Audrey. Your fucking crow has been causing problems, too."

I swallow hard, trying to think of what I can do to save my family. Before I can open my mouth, Luna speaks.

"Leave them be, mortal. It's me you want. I go willingly."

"Luna!" I gasp at the same time several witches enter the room. They pause over the body on the floor. One bends down and I see my father's hand reach up to her. It barely moves, but it means he's still alive, at least. Thank you, Goddess.

"What happened here?" The woman calls out in a sharp tone.

"Nothing."

"You'd attack one of your own?" She marches across the room and a bright light flashes. The man shrieks, holding his arm as he scowls at the woman.

"You struck me!" he hisses.

"You've nearly killed one of your brothers, I don't want to hear a word about it. Get out. It's time to take the Celestial upstairs."

Luna tilts her chin up with pride as they loosen her bindings and haul her from the chair. Again, I struggle with the ropes, even as Beezlebub gnaws away at them.

"Luna!" I cry out, my chest heavy.

She looks over her shoulder and smiles as they drag her up the stairs. She smiles. Why would she do that?

"I need to check on your father, Alandra," Mom whimpers from her seat as the door closes.

"B is trying to get these ropes off me, I think."

"He's going to die. Alandra, I have to put pressure on the wound. There's spirits around him, please," she begs, her eyes welling up with tears.

I flex my wrists, trying to gauge the condition of the ropes. They seem the least bit looser. If I can just—I pull my wrists apart as hard and fast as I can and my eyes pop open when they snap.

"B!" I squeal. "Thank you, thank you, thank you!" I rush over to my mom and begin working at the knots that hold her. It takes a few tries but eventually they come free. She rubs her wrists as she darts across the room to Dad.

I move to Laney next, pulling at the ropes that hold her. My fingers itch in a strange way and I shake my head. The ropes must be spelled. That's how they've been keeping her locked away so thoroughly. I back away from the chair, glancing toward Mom where she hovers over Dad, pressing on his stomach.

A loud groan comes from him and as bad as I feel for him, I'm grateful, because it means he's still breathing.

"I can't get Laney's ropes off, they're spelled."

"Use your shirt," Mom replies, as if that were an obvious answer.

I scrunch my nose up but quickly shrug out of my hoodie and shirt, using the thinner material like a glove as I tug and pull at the knots keeping my sister unconscious.

Beezlebub lights onto my bare shoulder and I bite my lip, trying to get the last piece of rope to budge and finally, it falls free. I move around to the front of the chair, pulling my shirt on as I go. I shake Laney's knee and smack the outside of her thigh. "Hey, wake up. Laney!"

She moans in her sleep—the first sound I've heard from her since we got here, whenever that was—and I quickly pull my hoodie back on and begin tapping her cheeks.

"Time to wake up, sis," I mumble before smacking her cheek hard enough to leave red print.

"What the fuck!" she hollers as she jumps awake. Small fires erupt around her and I dance backwards, narrowly avoiding one.

"It's me!" I squeak, shoving my hands into my hoodie pockets. The fires go out as recognition flashes across her face.

"Oh Goddess," she mutters, looking around the room while she rubs her temples. "My head. Where's Mom? Where's Luna?"

I point where Mom is bent over Dad near the fire and Laney jumps up, just to stumble back into her chair.

"Easy. You've been out for a while."

"Help me," she whispers and I nod. I slide my arm under her shoulder and around her back and we make our way across the room to our parents.

"What happened to him?" she asks, blinking away confused tears.

Dad shakes his head and holds out a hand. "I'm so sorry," he mutters.

"Shh," Laney gasps, wiping at her face. "It's going to be okay. Mom let go." She never takes her eyes off Dad as she places her own hand over the wound. Her hands glow an odd shade of orange and then the screaming starts.

"Agh!" Dad cries out, over and over, bucking against Laney's hands. Mom moves to hold his shoulders still and I grab his legs. She really should have told us what she was about to do but to her credit, she did just wake up. Bile rises in my throat as the scent of burnt flesh hits my nose.

"Goddess, the smell," I manage between gags.

"Almost. Done." Laney's brows cinch together, sweat beading on her forehead as she makes one final push against his stomach then leans back.

I move quickly to stop her from hitting the floor. She's weak as hell, barely any strength left after being bound and then doing . . . whatever she just did. "Where the fuck did you learn to do that?"

"I don't know," she admits with a chuckle. "I hope it worked."

My eyes flick to Dad's sweat drenched body. His color is all wrong, much paler than normal, but the wound is no longer bleeding, at least. I look to Mom, a question on my lips that I don't want to ask.

"I don't know," she says, as if reading my mind. And maybe she did. I've never understood how her powers work. Despite what the human movies may lead people to believe, mediums are exceedingly rare.

"What do we do, now?" My heart pounds against my chest. "If no one came during all that screaming . . ." I can't bring myself to finish the sentence. Worry for Luna turns my stomach and all the bile I choked down while Laney worked on Dad threatens to resurface.

"You have to go to her," Mom whispers. "You're right. The only reason we haven't been flooded with your father's idiotic friends is because they must be too close to the apex of the ritual to care what's going on down here. You'll never forgive yourself if you don't try." Mom smiles sadly at me.

"What the hell am I supposed to do!?" My voice is a strained whisper-yell as panic settles in my stomach. I have no active power and no more hexbags. There's nothing me and my moth can do against a coven of dark witches.

"I'll go with you," Laney says.

"You can barely walk." I shake my head, dragging my fingers through my hair as I try to reason out a solution.

"I don't have to walk to set shit on fire. Just get me up the stairs, Bug."

My eyes widen and Mom nods, closing her eyes. "I'll stay with your Dad. Give them hell, girls."

My hands shake as I pull Laney to her feet. In the corner, a case of water sits, half empty and I steady her before dashing for a bottle. Or three. I toss one to Mom and hand one to Laney as I take a few sips myself. They haven't been taking care of us like they should. I feel like there should be some kind of rules if you're holding prisoners, about how to treat them. The humans have something like that, don't they?

Oh right. The Geneva Convention.

I roll my eyes as the realization sets in that we really are less civilized than our less talented cousins. It's sad, really. Laney chugs the entire bottle of water before I'm able to screw the cap back on my own and my jaw gapes.

"You okay?" I ask again, skeptical of her ability to get up the stairs.

"I will be. Thank you." She tosses the bottle into the fire and takes one shaky step toward the stairs. My hand hovers at her back, scared she might fall over, but she seems a little more steady after the water.

"Don't fall on me, woman," I hiss as we reach the bottom of the stairs.

"No promises."

My mouth goes dry as we take one step, then another, up the dark stairway toward the creepy house above.

"I'm going to light them up. Have you seen Juney?" Laney whispers. Beezlebub nuzzles against my ear and I shake my head.

"The guy who hurt Dad had claw marks on his face. I don't know where she is. He said the familiars were creating problems, so I guess Brenna is out there too, causing chaos."

We pause at a door. What kind of basement has two doors? Laney and I exchange a look before I twist the knob slowly. The door swings open and no one jumps out at us. My heart hammers in my chest, waiting for the other shoe to drop but Laney pushes past me and steps out onto the creaky wooden floor first, a small fireball in her palm.

"Careful," I hiss, as she starts to wobble.

"I'll be fine."

We're in what looks like a living room. Old furniture covered in dusty sheets litters the room in a haphazard arrangement. Listening carefully, I strain my ears trying to hear anything but there's nothing. No one is in this damn house but us.

Beezlebub flits away toward the open door and I look toward Laney. She shrugs and we follow him out onto the porch. In the yard, a circle of witches surround Luna. There's so many of them, they loop around her twice. Quiet chanting floats to my ears. I have no idea what they're saying. It's old magic in a language I've never heard spoken. Is there a language older than Latin?

"When they scatter, get her," Laney whispers, bracing her hips against the rickety porch. She raises both hands into the air and tosses me a wink before fire erupts from both palms.

Chapter 25

Alandra

Most of the chanting comes to a stop, replaced by screams and shouts as flames erupt on two sides of the circle. The flames burn higher and higher as Laney stares down the coven of witches. My heart hammers in my chest, urging me to do something, anything.

But I don't have that kind of magic.

As witches from the outermost ring turn and run toward the porch, Laney splits her attention and sets a few cloaks on fire. They stop moving toward us and she smirks, leaning heavily on the railing.

"They're not running," I mutter in frustration.

"Give it time." The flames burn higher, pushing in toward the witches who are closest to Luna. One screams out as flames begin to lick their skin. Several witches abandon the circle and begin retreating into the woods.

"Do not abandon your Order!" a deep male voice shouts. Goosebumps blast across the back of my neck as I hone in on whoever that voice belongs to.

That has to be their leader. The one standing directly in front of Luna, hands on either side of her face, head thrown back as if gazing at the moon.

"Luna!" I scream as her head falls back and white light—moonlight—flows freely from her eyes and mouth. I rush down the stairs, pushing past the few remaining witches in the outer ring, I try to shoulder myself through the inner ring. I have to get to her.

Flames erupt around me and move with me as I push past witch after witch. *Holy fuck, my sister is a badass.* When I push against a body, their cloak burns. I glance down at myself, wondering how Laney can do this without hurting me, but don't have time to question it as a large witch turns and begins lopping bolts of electricity at me. I throw my hands up to block the blow, but the moment the electricity sinks into my veins, I feel my heart veins constrict. The jolt rushes to the center of me, knocking me onto my back.

I blink, a stuttered groan spilling from my lips as the larger man bends over me. As his face pushes closer to mine, I take a deep breath, trying to hold onto consciousness.

"You Michaels don't know when to stop, do you?" he sneers, opening his palm as if to summon more magic.

Before he can deal the final blow, flames arc up and down his arms and his face twists in pain. "Ah!" he screams, patting at his skin, but it's too late. The fire spreads along his cloak, engulfing him in a blaze so hot it's nearly blue.

"Leave her be!" Laney shouts from the porch, sending another wave of fire toward the circle. Several witches catch flame. I struggle to my feet, trying to regain my wits and watch the mayhem around me.

Burning witches flee their position in the circle, and as soon as they abandon their post, the flames attacking them disappear. Laney isn't trying to kill them, she's just trying to stop this.

I push past the remains of the man before me. I feel no guilt for his death. He would have killed me. I was already on the ground, stunned beyond belief. Another blow could have stopped my heart. Actually, I'm surprised the first few didn't. As I step over his body, my eyes fall on Luna. Three witches remain around the inner circle, their cloaks engulfed in flames, but they're rooted in place.

For a moment, I wonder if they're this dedicated to their cause or if their leader is preventing them from leaving somehow. From the screams piercing the night, I'd bet money on the latter.

Tentatively, I step into the ring and move behind the leader. *Great Goddess, help me.* Unable to think clearly, I decide on going old school and just rush the fucker. I spear him with my arms around his waist and try to tackle him to the ground. Surprisingly, he does fall with me to the side of Luna.

During the struggle, he manages to get on top of me, his knees digging into my thighs. His hand wraps around my throat as I see his face clearly for the first time. Wrinkled skin hangs loosely from his cheeks and green eyes bore into mine. "You fucking fool, the transfer has already begun."

"T—transfer?" I choke out, scrabbling at his hand. Pressure against my windpipe makes it hard to breathe and harder to speak. A line of fire streams toward him, but he flicks it away.

Laney's frustrated scream sounds behind me.

Blast after blast of fire rains down around us. The heat brushes against my skin, but the fire never touches me. The witch holding me to the ground snarls as he deflects each attack, clearly losing patience. The strength of the blasts grows stronger just as dark spots crowd in around the edges of my vision. I'm going to pass out soon.

"Get off of her!" Laney snarls. A high pitched snarl tears through the night at the same time the man screams out in pain.

I scramble away from him, my hand going to my throat protectively as I watch Juniper sink her teeth into his leg again. The momentary break in concentration means he misses the next stream of fire. His cloak bursts into flames but he manages to shrug out of it before he's engulfed.

White light begins to pool in his green eyes, filling him with Luna's power and I shake my head. *No.* A few feet away, Luna sits on her knees, arms spread out, face tilted up to the sky as energy pours out of her.

"I tried to tell you," he sneers. A sickening sound of crunching bone rings out through the clearing and I twist around, trying to find my sister.

Laney collapses onto the snow-covered ground, her fingers digging into the cold earth as tears pour down her face. Another snap makes her scream.

"Stop it!" I scream, rising to my feet. The witches who remain are charred to a crisp, but rooted in place, unable to move. "You sacrificed your own coven for this power?" I ask, gesturing to the grotesquely displayed corpses.

He snaps a finger and their remains crumple into dust.

"Prather, stop this," a male voice calls out from the porch. I turn to see Dad, heavily support by Mom, walking toward us. He flicks his wrist and I watch as the man before me twitches involuntarily.

"It won't work," Prather replies, holding a hand out in my direction. "I have too much of the Celestial's power, now, Michaels."

"Leave my daughter alone. Let us leave," he groans as mom rushes from his side to the place where Laney lay in the snow, sobbing.

"I can't do that now." In the split second it takes Prather to level his eyes on my father, I dart for Luna. I don't know that anything I do will matter, but I have to.

If this is our ending, I want to spend it with her.

My fingers brush against her shoulders as my arms go around her neck. She doesn't respond. Her head is trapped in an awkward position as her light pours out of her and into the night. Somehow Prather is siphoning every bit of her into himself.

"I'm so sorry," I whisper with a thick tongue, my tears falling against her neck. "I tried, love."

"Prather don't!" Someone calls out. I can't make out who the voice belongs to. My eyes snap open at the same time something goes wrong in my spine.

It doesn't hurt.

There's no pain.

There's only a cold numbness sweeping throughout my body. As I lose the ability to support myself, my weight around Luna's neck brings her face crashing down toward mine. Our eyes collide and I'm lost in the moonlight spilling out of her.

Drowned in the sound of a thousand whispered prayers and rituals. Even the very chant that's ending her life rings in my ears.

I BLINK OPEN MY EYES AND PANIC SEIZES MY BODY. QUICKLY, I scramble to my feet just realize there is no ground beneath me. I turn in a circle, examining where I am and my stomach falls into a bottomless pit as I gaze at a million shining stars.

"Be still, mortal," a soothing voice calls out from the darkness.

I squint my eyes against the light as she appears. Her hair is like molten gold, flowing down her bronze skin. She wears no clothing to cover her heavy breasts or swollen stomach. Her eyes mirror the black space and stars that surround us.

"Am I dead?" I ask before I think better of it. I know who she is, but I can't wrap my mind around the absurdity.

"Not quite yet, it would seem." The Great Goddess waves a hand toward an empty space near us and a vision of Luna on her knees, her power pouring into . . . me . . . springs to life.

"Is this real? Am I there or here? Is Luna alive?" My stomach clenches at the thought of her death. It scares me more than being faced with my own.

"Slow down, child," the Goddess laughs. "You are in both places, currently. Your physical being is on what you call Earth, with your arms wrapped around my daughter. Your spiritual being has been sent here, to me, to consider."

"To consider?" I ask, rubbing my temples. I should have paid much closer attention in school. It's obvious something big is happening but I don't understand what.

"Yes," she murmurs, taking a step toward me. The Great Goddess clasps her hands at her waist before continuing. Gold and white light flares shimmer behind her, as if coming from her back, and maybe they are. "An evil man has absorbed some of my daughter's power. He means to drain her and use the power for his own purposes. You don't want this to happen."

It wasn't a question, so I don't speak. The Great Goddess inclines her head with a sly smile.

"You have absorbed the rest of Luna's power, but only after receiving your death blow."

I swallow hard as an ache begins to throb in my back, as if her speaking the words reminded my body that it should be hurting. "So I am dead, then."

"Not quite yet. Your soul brought you here, to me. Do you know why?" Her black eyes twinkle with the light of a thousand stars and I shake my head.

"I don't."

"Do you remember the last thing you asked of me, Alandra Michaels?"

My brow creases. I rack my brain trying to remember if I asked the Goddess for anything. I don't usually pray—

"I asked you to save Luna and my father." I cover my mouth, looking back to the vision of me and Luna. I know it's not physical. I know I can't touch her, but I want to rush to her and say goodbye.

"Yes. And then this happened." The Great Goddess waves her hand and a scene plays out against the stars around us, as if they're a projector screen. I see myself run toward Luna, throw my arms around her neck, and Prather slings his hand out toward me. My back arches at an unnatural angle and I crumple backward, my arms still locked around Luna's neck. Her head falls forward and energy pours from her body into mine before my body goes limp.

"Is my family okay?" I ask, quietly.

"For now. Though, your sister may never be the same after the pain this Prather subjected her to."

My heart twists in my chest at those words. Laney already struggles with addiction. I worry she won't be able to climb out of this hole after the amount of trauma she was subject to.

"You are a very good witch, Alandra Michaels."

I snort, then cover my mouth, my eyes wide with horror. "I am so sorry."

The Great Goddess shakes her head and laughs, her chest heaving with each chuckle. "It is, as you say, alright, child. You are a very good witch in the sense that you have a very good heart. Do you know your power?"

I blink and shake my head. "I have none."

"You are wrong."

My heart hammers against my chest as The Great Goddess comes forward and presses a finger to my forehead. "You are a vessel."

My brow wrinkles under her attention. "I don't know what that means."

"I know. Your people have forgotten the value of vessels over the last few millennia. Vessels once lead your people. You are a source of magic and can hold it within you without being changed by its fabric."

The words sound foreign to me, as if they don't translate well. I take a deep breath and nod, accepting that tidbit for whatever it may mean. "Does this mean I can save Luna?"

"And that, my child, is why you are a good witch." The Great Goddess nods and shows me another image, one of Prather wrenching my hands off Luna and throwing us both to the ground. My own dead eyes reflect pure moonlight back to him as he rages into the night.

"Should you return to Earth and manage to absorb the rest of my daughter's power from this vile creature, you could return it to her. If you so choose."

"If I return to Earth?" I ask, confused.

"There is another option. One you might prefer." The Great Goddess bows her head and suddenly I'm in a familiar dream, surrounded by tall purple grass and silver blossoms. "You have enough of Luna's power to take her place, if you so wish. It will take you a few centuries to cultivate the power to the level needed to rule this realm, but it is doable."

My fingers drift along the top of the grass to a closed blossom. As I touch it, it unfolds, glowing white in the center. *Moon blossoms.* "This is where Luna lives."

"Yes."

The power coursing inside me finally registers as the blossoms all begin to open. I can feel them like they're a part of me. I shake my head and back away, the blossoms closing as I disconnect from them mentally. "How do I go home?"

"You need only ask. Your mortal form will be changed by your visit to this realm. I'm not sure what that means for you in the future, but there is no visiting this world and leaving untouched."

I take a deep breath and nod then bow carefully to show my respect. "Thank you, Great Goddess. Please, take me home."

The last thing I see in the darkness is her brilliant smile.

Chapter 26

Alandra

My eyes fly open and air surges into my lungs. It feels like fire consuming me from the inside out. Choking on the precious oxygen, I blink away my tears as the night sky comes into view.

Oh no, did I not make it back?

"You killed her!" a familiar voice roars. Quiet sobbing drifts to me from somewhere nearby.

"You could have been a God, Michaels," Prather hisses. I raise slowly and look down at Luna's lifeless body. Her glow is completely gone. There's not a single shimmer to light up the snow around her.

As my stomach clenches and tears threaten to fill my eyes, a quiet voice whispers in the back of my mind. *You can save her, child. Remember what must be done.* I blink away the moisture and nod, steeling myself against what's to come. I turn and face Prather's back. His skin glows—not as brightly as my Luna's—in the darkness. Beyond him, Laney sits cradled in my mother's lap, holding her leg and arm at awkward angles.

Rage boils deep in my chest as he lifts his hand in the air. My father's eyes go wide when he sees me, but I'm focused on Prather. All the rage I've ever felt pools in my fingertips and erupts in the form of energy.

Prather falls to the ground and slides a few feet in the snow, revealing the dead grass beneath it as he goes.

"How fucking dare you!" I scream, marching toward him with my hands raised. The power coursing through my body is new, foreign, and I have no idea how to control it. Another stream of energy comes from my hands toward him, but he throws his own up and blocks it.

We have the same magic, now.

"How is this possible? You're dead. I killed you." He scrambles to his feet, his eyes wide with fear as he backs further away from me.

"Yes, you did. It would seem I suck at dying too," I snap. The water in the snow around us calls to me, to the power trapped inside me. I raise my hands, palm up, then push toward Prather as a wall of snow forms and topples around him. "Leave my family alone!"

Prather shakes and the snow falls to the ground as a cruel smile twists his lips. "The little null finally has power. You must be so proud, Michaels," he spits.

"I'm not a fucking null, you murderous piece of shit!" A feral scream rips from my throat as I run toward him. Pure instinct. That's the only way I can describe the decision to charge directly toward a man who outmatches me magically and is nearly twice my size, even if his age takes away some of his advantage.

He squares his stance, waiting for me to spear him like I did before, but I've learned that lesson. Trusting the power rushing through my veins, I take a step on nothing but air and then another until I'm close enough to do what I want. My body falls through the air, my foot slamming into his jaw as we both plummet to the ground.

Prather roars in pain and rage as we scramble for the upper hand. His hands come around my throat and a feeling of deja vu slides over me. My fingers dig into the snow around us and I call to it, asking it to help me.

Slender ropes of snow form and crawl around his body like living ropes. They creep around his neck, his hands, his chest—everywhere that might give some tactical advantage—and then they solidify to ice.

"Gods be," he mutters, struggling against his icy chains, but they don't budge. My heart hammers against my chest as I try to remember what the Great Goddess said about absorbing the power from him.

It's yours, call it to you. Quick, before he figures out the same.

My hands cup his cheeks as I stare into his eyes, trying to recreate the way I ended up with Luna's power. "You are mine, come to me," I whisper.

"No!" Prather struggles against his bonds, the ice creaking and groaning under his weight. They won't last much longer. My nails dig into his skin as I focus on pulling all of my power back to me. White moonlight seeps from his eyes and pours into me. Shivers of excitement rush through my body as all the power settles deep into my core.

Is this what Luna feels like all the time?

It's mind boggling. I feel like I could conquer the universe if I wanted. But, luckily, I'm not Prather and that's not what I want. When the last bit of moonlight slides inside me, I focus on pulling any residual energy inside him.

He doesn't deserve to wield magic as a weapon against his own people.

Prather coughs, his eyes going wide with fresh tears as a soft, purple smoke gurgles from his lips. It worms its way between mine and I stiffen for a moment as the unusual sensation flows through my being.

When it's done I push away from him and stand, looking down at my shimmering hands. "Now you're a null. Don't ever come near my family again. If you do, you'll lose more than magic."

His lip shakes as he looks down at his own hands. "No . . ."

I turn to face my family and my father takes a step back. "Wh—what are you, Alandra?"

"Nothing for long." I turn to Laney to see if she's okay.

"Don't worry about me," she whimpers before I can even open my mouth. "Luna."

I nod and rush to where Luna lays in the snow, her eyes fixed on the dark night sky. As I kneel over her, I slip my hands under her head and whisper.

"Please come back to me. Take what's yours. The magic. Me. Just come back," I murmur quietly so only she and the Great Goddess can hear. The light doesn't burst painfully from my eyes like I expect it to. Instead, it seeps slowly into her body where my hand meet her skin. I slide one hand against her cheek and fresh tears fall down my cheeks as the shimmer begins to spread beneath her skin.

"That's it," I whisper. "Come back."

Thank you...

The whisper in the back of my mind is so faint I can't be sure if I heard it at all. Or maybe the magic leaving my body has something to do with why she sounds so quiet, but her voice fades into nothing as Luna takes her first breath in my arms.

"Oh Goddess, thank you," I whisper against her hair as I bring her against my chest.

Luna mumbles something sleepily against my chest but I just squeeze her harder, thankful she's alive.

"Landra wer oven me," she mumbles, whatever words she intends to say coming out a garbled mess. Oh Goddess, did something go wrong when she came back? I push away from her and look down at her pale eyes in question.

"You're smothering me," she coughs out with a weak smile.

"Oh, shit. Shit! I'm sorry!" I squeak, backing up an inch.

"Thank you," she murmurs, sitting up on her own. Luna throws her arms around my neck and squeezes me, holding me tight against her. When she pulls away from the hug, my heart dips but not for long. Her mouth crashes down on mine in a hungry kiss. Her lips pull at my own as her tongue slides into my mouth to claim me.

I nearly fall back into the snow as her weight wars with my own. Tilting my head to the side to deepen the kiss, a soft tickle at my neck brings me back to reality.

"Ahhh!" I squeal against her mouth, backing up to see what's crawling on me.

Beezlebub chitters angrily from his place on my chest and I snicker as his antennae and feet rub together like some kind of threat. "I'm sorry!" I answer. I have no idea what he's 'saying', but he seems pissed.

"You scared him."

"I scared *me*," I laugh. "Hell, *you* scared me."

The soft sound of someone clearing their throat brings my attention to my freezing, injured family. I pull a face and then look back at Luna. "Would you heal them if I asked?"

"Anything for you."

I look up at the sky as we stand to our feet, noting the moon's position. "You're not trapped here anymore," I whisper, a sense of dread constricting my throat.

"No." Luna walks slowly toward my family and I take a deep breath, preparing myself for what's to come.

I knew what would happen when we began this. I knew this couldn't go anywhere. I just need to remind myself of that. It's the trauma. I'm overreacting because of the trauma. Not because I'm an emotional mess. As we get close to them, I wave my hand at Laney where she lays in the snow. Luckily her fire magic makes it hard for her to get cold. As my wave comes to an end, a small line swipes through the snow toward her and she raises her eyebrow.

"What was that?"

"Uh." I look down at my hand and shrug, then flick it again in her direction. A larger dollop of snow slams against her chest.

"Bug..."

"You have Prather's telekinesis," Dad offers from the side.

I round on him, my eyes wide. I don't know what I want to say to him. He's... my dad. But he also tried to kill my girlfriend. And he's alienated me for most of my life for not being good enough.

"Alandra," Mom whispers and I turn to her, deciding to leave the confrontation with my dad for another time. From the corner of my eye, I can see his shoulders slump. His hand covers the wound at his stomach, causing a fresh surge of guilt to spring up in my chest.

"Are you okay?" I ask, even as my eyes drift to Laney. The sound of bones snapping back together as Luna heals her makes me cringe. The quiet hisses and cries of pain as her bones stitch themselves back together is heart wrenching.

"I'm okay. Honey, look at me," Mom begs quietly. My eyes rise to meet hers and I sigh under the weight of the night. "It's okay. You got the girl, baby," she whispers.

"Everything isn't magically going to be okay," I sigh, nodding my head toward Dad tying up Prather with his own magic.

"I—I know. He knows, too. When the hunters come, your dad is going to go willingly. He needs to pay for the things he's done." Mom sniffs, a sad smile pulling up her lips.

"Really?" I ask, turning to watch him as he plops down in the snow beside his former leader.

"Really. He promised when he woke up inside, before you. . . before you died. If he goes back on it, I'll testify against him myself. He needs to pay for all the ways he's hurt our community and our family." Mom turns to Luna and shakes her head. "And you, sweetheart. I'm so sorry for the things you were put through."

Luna's hands pause on Laney's stomach—likely healing a broken rib—and she nods solemnly. "Thank you."

Everything still isn't okay, but I won't repeat it. The fact he's willing to take responsibility for his actions speaks volumes.

"Luna," Mom whispers, her eyes going soft for a moment. "When the hunters get here . . . it's best if you aren't. We don't know how many other dark covens there are." Mom swallows hard.

A rock forms in the pit of my stomach as Luna stands and helps Laney to her feet. Panic shoots through my chest as I wait for the words that will break me.

"Alright, Audrey, I'll go."

I swallow again, fighting the tears brimming in the corner of my eyes. This was what was always going to happen. In the corner of my eye, Laney covers her mouth, but I can't bear to look her in the eyes. I can't bear the 'I told you so'.

"Come, love," Luna commands, and my head snaps up in question.

"What?" Mom, Laney, and I ask at the same time.

"Come with me. If you want." Luna's eyes never leave mine, her chest rising and falling with each breath.

"Alandra, you can't, you—"

"Yes," I murmur quietly, searching her eyes for something. What, I don't know.

It was never a question. This world has never been mine. My family hasn't ever wanted me, apart from Laney. My parents have never been satisfied with who I am, or what I am. Even if Dad takes the hunters' punishment on the chin and comes out a better person . . . it doesn't undo the years of emotional torture I've suffered at their hands.

Forgive them, but live your life thoroughly.

My eyebrows cinch together and Luna smiles at me warmly. "You hear her?"

"Yes."

"You'll have to tell me what you and the Great Mother discussed, love." Luna takes my hand and squeezes it before stepping away, presumably to give me a moment to say my goodbyes.

"Alandra," Mom hisses quietly. "You can't go with her. You're a mortal, what would you do in the Celestial realm? What would you become?"

"I don't know. I'm still going." I beam up at her and throw my arms around her neck in a fierce hug, soaking up her scent. "I can still come home. Witches can't cross into the Celestial realm uninvited, that doesn't mean Celestials can't cross over, if they choose. I promise I'll come back."

"Bug," Laney whimpers, sniffling as tears run freely down her face. "Tonight? You have to go to tonight?"

"I want to. It's not safe for her here. And I don't want to be apart from her, Laney," I sigh. "Can you forgive me?"

Her eyes fall but she nods, wiping at her tears before she throws her arms around me next. Her inner fire warms me to my bones before I step back. Dad sits by a gagged Prather—really, where did he find something to gag him with?—with a sad smile on his face.

I take a hesitant step toward him, trying to fight the anger in my gut. "I'm leaving," I mumble.

"I heard."

"Alright then," I sigh, turning back toward Luna.

"Wait," he calls out and I pause, looking over my shoulder. "I always just wanted what's best for you, Alandra. I hope you know that."

"No," I growl, shaking my head. Beezlebub flies toward Dad, chittering angrily in his face as if he wants to give him a piece of his mind, too. "You wanted what was best for you and your image. You think I didn't hear what your buddy said? 'The little null finally has power'. I know what you think of me, Dad. I've always known." My hand shakes as it rises and points in Luna's direction. "I'm going to go and make a life for myself that doesn't involve your judgment. I told Mom

I'll visit, and I will. Whether or not you see me depends entirely upon how much you've changed by then."

My father's eyes go wide as I turn around and stomp toward the white haired beauty waiting for me. As my hand slides into hers, Beezlebub comes and clings carefully to the fabric of my hoodie.

"Don't worry little guy," Luna coos. "The journey won't hurt at all."

"I love you!" Mom calls out in a worried voice.

"Me too, Bug!"

I squeeze Lunas hand and call over my shoulder, "Love you."

Luna presses against the air and a shimmer ripples outwards until a large oval hangs in front of us. Every color—plus a few new ones, I think—swirls inside and I swallow hard, running my free hand over Beezlebub's back.

"Trust me," Luna whispers, stepping through the door to her realm.

As if there were ever any question.

I take a deep breath and follow her into the unknown.

Epilogue

I try to roll over, attempting to untangle myself from the mess of limbs I find myself in. Luna is wrapped around me like a spider monkey, clinging so tightly I can barely move.

"Luna," I whisper, patting her arm.

"Mm."

"Luna," I try again with a smile.

This time her arms loosen and I roll over, my head sliding against the smooth silk pillowcase as I come face to face with my consort.

"Good morning, Little Witch," she mumbles with a groggy voice.

I snicker, poking her face in the annoying way she hates as Elysium songs drift to my ears through the open window. Well, it's not exactly a window. Our home has no doors or windows. No barriers of any kind. Even the walls are made from some strange, clear stone. There's no rain or storms in this realm. Only peaceful breezes drift through our bedroom occasionally, bringing the prayers and spellwork of other witches with it.

"You realize that time works differently here, Little Witch," she groans, pulling a pillow over her head. "We don't have to rush."

"I know, but I want to see Laney. I miss her." I poke out my bottom lip out and bat my eyelashes. Luna peeks out from beneath the pillow with a small smirk and quickly leans up, brushing her lips over mine.

"Fine, fine," she sighs. "We'll leave early. I don't know why you guilt me, though. You saw her just last week."

"I'm used to seeing her every day."

I hope that one day the mortal realm will be safe enough for Luna and I stay longer, but for now, we visit when we can. I worry about Laney living alone. She dumped Marcus during the Luna drama and as far as I know, hasn't been dating anyone since.

"Stop fretting," Luna whispers, pulling me into a tight hug. "It will be fine, whatever it is."

"One of these days I'll get used to that," I sigh happily into her neck as I soak up the embrace. Her empathic abilities still catch me off guard sometimes. Even though Luna has been sharing her power with me, a little at a time, I have such a small understanding of how it truly works.

"Mm," Luna hums noncommittally. With a snap of her fingers, her favorite sheer dress—and, admittedly, my favorite to see her in—is replaced with something a little more appropriate for my family's Beltane feast. The white dress with silver lace accents and silver buttons hugs every curve of her body.

She rises to her feet and looks me over before snapping her fingers again. I glance down to the swooping neckline. The silver cloth clings tight to my breasts. As I swing my legs over the edge of the bed, I quickly realize the rest of the outfit is fairly loose. Billowing fabric hangs around my hips and legs then comes to a tight closer just above my ankles.

"A genie jumper?" I ask with a grin.

"A what?" Luna's eyebrows cinch together as she examines the outfit. "You don't like it?"

"It's wonderful, love," I laugh. "Very beautiful."

Luna crosses the room and wraps her arms around my neck, peering down at me with her silver eyes.

"It's beauty belongs to you, Little Witch."

"I like the sound of that," I snicker as I tilt my head back for one more kiss. Luna obliges, leaning down to press her lips to mine. I suck her bottom lip between my teeth, teasing her with the tip of my tongue before I pull away.

"Alandra," she whispers in warning.

"Do you think I can open portals yet?" I ask, ignoring the sound of her palpable frustration.

"You could try," she sighs, spinning me around by my shoulders until my back is pressed to her chest. "Press your hands against the air," she instructs, rubbing her hands down my arms until she's holding my wrists loosely.

I do as she says, pushing into the air until I feel something solid beneath my fingertips.

"Ah! Is that the ether?" A quiet chittering tickles my ears as Beezlebub lands on my shoulder. This realm had been kind to him. The light reflected beautifully off his markings, revealing depth in his patterns that I never knew existed before coming here.

"Probably," she laughs. "Now imagine where you want to be, and press until it opens for you."

"Like a door," I muse, pushing against the ether until it began to part. As the first few sparks of color fly out from the small portal, I let out a tiny excited squee.

"Precisely like a door." Luna kisses my cheek gently as we both watch the portal grow in size. When it's big enough to walk through, she links her fingers through mine and casts a worried glance at the portal. "You made sure to think of your old home? Yes?"

"Of course," I laugh. "If this works like you said, then it should take us to my old bedroom."

"Mmm," Luna hums, tapping her chin with her free hand. "Alright, Little Witch. Let's go."

We step through the portal and once again I'm entranced by the swirling colors as we're pulled toward our destination as Beezlebub's furry legs scramble for a better hold on my shoulder. The light changes around us until we're deposited into the corner of a familiar room. Beezlebub instantly flies from my shoulder and around my old bedroom while a grin stretches my face.

"You did it," Luna purrs.

"Bug?" a familiar voice calls out from somewhere on the other side of the open door. My eyebrow arches as I pull Luna toward the hallway.

"We're here!"

"Bug!" Laney squeals as she slides to a stop in the hallway. Her arms wrap me in a fierce hug and I twist my fingers free from Luna's to embrace her properly.

"Goddess, you're excited."

"Well—Hi luna!—I have news." Laney slips her arm through mine and half drags me down the hallway with Luna chuckling behind us.

"Hello Laney," she laughs.

"What news?" I ask suspiciously. "How's Mom?"

"Mom's great," Laney answers quickly as we reach the living room. "And the hunters are going to release Dad in June. Mom has been doing a lot of research about Vessels. She's had all her ghosty friends trying to figure out how your powers work. Dad says he doesn't have the right to comment on your magic bec—"

"He's right," I growl. "He doesn't. Why are they letting him out early?" My eyes flick to Luna whose face is completely passive. She'd decided months ago to stay out of the family drama, if at all possible. Supposedly, she didn't hold any ill will toward my Dad about the sacrifice attempt because, and I quote, *"He realized he was wrong."*

"Bug, he feels awful," Laney whispers, tucking a long strand of raven colored hair behind her ear. She's been letting it grow back out. She was cute with a pixie-cut, but the longer hair suits her.

"I know. He should." I can't help the anger boiling in my stomach. Luna could preach forgiveness all she wanted, but I'm still angry. This lifelong resentment had been building to a crescendo for some time and *"I'm sorry,"* wasn't going to cut it.

"Little Witch," Luna calls out, her voice tense.

"Bug, you have to forgive them eventually. They do love you," Laney insists, ignoring Luna.

I narrow my eyes on my sister and turn my head over my shoulder to find Luna staring at the window with a puzzled expression. "What's wrong, love?"

"I think your mother's here."

Just then, the door swings open and Mom walks in, holding out her arms. I go to her and wrap her in a hug.

"Hey, Mom," I murmur.

The quiet sounds of Luna and Laney chattering behind us interrupts the silent moment. Mom gives me one final squeeze before taking a step back so she can get a look at me.

"Lord, power suits you," she admits with a shy smile.

"Mom," I groan, pressing my palm to my forehead.

"It's true! Come, sit, you need to see something on TV." Mom rushes away from me and begins fiddling with the remote, changing the channel over and over until she finds the correct one. She sinks into the couch and pats the cushions beside her. "Come on, girls, all three of you."

Luna snickers, obviously amused by something, but she's the first to move to sit down. Laney and I follow with puzzled looks. As our butts hit the cushion, the man on TV begins speaking, a look of shock across his face.

> "Today, we're witnessing history. Forty-two covens across the North America have been raided by the HPWA in the organizations largest collaborated sting operation ever."

The beady eyed witch on the screen begins explaining the history of the HPWA—Hunters Protecting Witches Association—and I turn toward Mom.

"What's this about?"

"Shh, just watch," she answers, reaching across Laney to pat my leg.

Luna's hand rests lightly on my right thigh as my eyes slowly move back to the television. Images flash across the screen of witches in red robes and black masks being escorted by hunters.

> "The Order has lost every foothold it had in this continent." The man takes a second to take a deep breath. "Dark witches have plagued our kind for as long as we have existed. They're the underbelly of the witching community and these arrests will make it a little easier for us to sleep at night."
>
> A fair haired woman beside him gapes openly at the papers in her hand. "I had no idea The Order still existed to this degree. What brought this on?"

"An informant, who has not been named for obvious reasons, was arrested during a recent attempt to sacrifice a Celestial."

"They brought a Celestial to Earth? That hasn't happened since the Golden Age!"

"It would seem so, Anna. In exchange for leniency, the informant supplied the HPWA with names and locations of all of the The Order's operations they were privy to."

"For more information on this monumental story, we have Paul Abernathy with the HPWA."

I TURN IN MY SEAT TO FACE MY MOM AND SISTER, MY MOUTH HANGING open. "Did Dad do this?"

Mom nods, tears building in the corners of her eyes. "He didn't do it for leniency, either. They got that wrong. He told the hunters he'd give them whatever information they needed to put a stop to The Order. They offered him a reduced sentence after."

"Wow," I whisper, my heart thudding in my chest. Maybe these months in confinement had changed him. Maybe he'd finally realized how fucked up he really was.

Beside me, Luna stares intently at the TV screen. The HWPA agent drones on and on about how the fight against The Order wasn't over, how they still have operations on other continents, but this was a significant blow to their organization.

A human activist spoke next about how cleaning up the underbelly of the witching community was always a good thing for Human-Witch relations.

"They care," Luna whispers quietly.

Mom and Laney stop speaking and turn toward Luna, watching her stare in wonder at the newscast.

"Of course they care, babe," I murmur, slipping my fingers between hers.

"No. When I was tied up—" Luna chokes on her own emotion and shakes her head. "Not all witches are like that."

"No, we're not," Mom agrees quietly.

"Your father is going to bring about the next Golden Age." Luna wraps an arm around my shoulders, bringing me into her side as we watch the humans and hunters discuss The Order on national television.

"What a strange thing," Laney points out. "I never thought I'd see the day anyone spoke about dark witches so publicly. It's weird, right?"

"It really is," I agree. "But I guess they're less of a threat now."

"What do you think will happen to them?" I ask Mom. "Do you think Dad will be safe?" A sudden fit of panic constricts my chest. He could be in danger if they find out he's the informant.

"Stop worrying, Little Witch," Luna commands. "Your father knew what he was doing when he did this. The Hunters will protect him."

"They will. He did this for you, Alandra. He feels awful for a lot of things, but he feels very guilty for what he almost let happen to Luna."

I nod slowly, blinking away the moisture gathering in the corner of my eyes. I'm not sure if I'll be able to forgive him, but I can at least work on our relationship. What he did is huge. He broke a covenant for me, for our family, for what's right. That's a big deal.

"Do you want to go see him?" Luna asks quietly, flipping her long pale hair over her shoulder.

"Not yet," I admit. "I need some time, I think, to process all of this. After the Beltane festival, maybe?"

Everyone nods their agreement as we watch the news break on TV. Names scroll across the bottom of the screen, famous witches involved with The Order.

"This is going to bring our community to its knees," Laney whispers reverently.

"We'll get through this. We don't need organizations like The Order representing us. Dark witches are like cancer." Mom's voice is firm, severe. "I couldn't be prouder of your father."

"In the meeeeeeantime," Laney giggles, obviously trying to lighten the mood. "There's someone I want you all to meet tonight."

"What? Who?" I narrow my eyes on my sister. She's always had shitty taste in men.

"His name is Apollo and he's—"

"Apologies. His name is *what*?" Luna asks, her voice shrill.

"Apollo..." Laney cants her head to the side, chewing her bottom lip. "Why?"

Luna and I exchange a worried glance as we raise from the couch. "Let's go meet Laney's new boyfriend," I mutter.

"Wait, how do you know Apollo?"

"*Who* is Apollo?" Mom asks as she follows suit. I shrug my shoulders nonchalantly. It's not my place to say.

During my stay in Luna's realm, I've met most of the Celestials. She called them to her realm to introduce me, in case they should ever drop in and find a mortal lurking around. She called it a safety measure.

I called it showing off.

One Celestial stuck out above the others though, a dark skinned man with red dreadlocks, flames arcing from one lock of hair to the other. He was beautiful, and troublesome, and Luna can't stand him.

He's the Sun.

And his name is Apollo.

"What are you two in a rush for?" Laney asks suspiciously as I pull on the door handle.

"I've been rushing Luna all morning to come for the Beltane festival. Come on. They're probably already dancing!"

"Do I have to dance?" Luna asks, a look of abject horror passing over her face.

"Yes." I nod my head quickly. The door opens and Beezlebub lands on my neck, chittering away. He always takes Luna's side. A low rumble coming from the ground catches my eye and I drop to my knees, rubbing my hands across Juniper's head. "Awe, hi girl! Did you miss me?"

She rubs her muzzle against my palm, the smallest growl passing her lips. I always liked to think of it as purring. As I stand to my feet and step out onto the stoop, the darkness of night washes over me.

Luna's realm has spoiled me. The soft twilight darkness of lights everything just perfectly there, bringing out all the shimmers of the muted color scheme.

After we all pile into Mom's car, I slide into the middle seat and lean my head on Luna's shoulder. "Do you think it's him?"

"After hearing the story of how we met? I'm sure it is." Luna's leg shakes as Mom backs out of the driveway.

I glance up into the rearview mirror to find Laney's eyes staring back at me, a scowl across her forehead. A small smile curves my lips and I nuzzle my head against Luna's shoulder.

For some reason, the idea of my sister unknowingly dating a Celestial after all the shit she gave me about summoning Luna, amuses the hell out of me.

Apollo has always been my most troublesome son.

Shivers blast down my spine as the Great Goddess's voice rings in my ears. I haven't heard her voice since the night I revived Luna.

Maybe it's a side effect of Luna sharing her power with me. Figuring out the right balance of borrowed magic has been an interesting experiment. Of course, I'd insisted I didn't need any, but Luna wouldn't hear it.

"You're my consort," she'd murmur, every time I objected the small stream of white light flowing into my body. *"It's the least I can do."*

"I love you," I whisper quietly, so only she will hear me.

"I love you too, Little Witch."

AFTERWORD

Dear Reader,

Thank you so much for taking the time to read Witching Moon. This story was itching to be written for a while. I'm so glad I finally set a date for it. If you enjoyed it, please consider leaving an honest review. Reviews help authors in more ways than you know. Not only do they let us know what we're doing right (and wrong), they also help boost your favorite books in the search algorithms for other readers to find. More readers means more books from your favorite authors.

Will Laney and Apollo get a story? I believe they will, likely at the end of 2020 or beginning of 2021. Their characters kept whispering to me as I was writing Luna and Alandra's story. Their story will also be able to be read as a standalone. Make sure to follow me on social media for updates on upcoming projects.

I hope you enjoyed the girls as much as I did. Their love story inspires me.

Poppy Woods

ACKNOWLEDGMENTS

Thank you to everyone who encouraged me to explore the lesfic genre, especially my current readers. When I asked if you would read something outside your norm, because the idea spoke to me, you said, "I'll give anything you write a try." And I can't ask for more than that.

Thank you to my wonderful PA MalMal. I couldn't get any of this done without her. Thank you for being such an amazing friend.

Thank you to every ARC reader, friend, and peer who read snippets and bounced ideas throughout the writing process. You guys are amazing.

Thank you.

ABOUT THE AUTHOR

When Poppy isn't arguing with fictional characters, she can usually be found chasing her four year old around their Georgia home. On of the off occasion that she isn't writing or momming, Poppy is usually reading. If you catch a Poppy in the wild, just remember: Cocktails and chocolate are valid forms of bribery!

Get Updates on Poppy's Work:

Join her Mailing List
Follow Poppy on Twitter
Follow Poppy on Instagram
Follow Poppy on Bookbub
Like Poppy on Facboook
Join her reader's group on Facebook

ALSO BY POPPY WOODS

The Unsung Veil Series:

A Call to Pride

A Call to Heart

A Call to War

Coming soon . . . A Call to Freedom (Ryan's Story)

Shipwreck Souls (Featuring K.A. Knight and Kendra Moreno)

The Dinoverse:

Dances with Raptors

Rexes and Robbers (By Kendra Moreno)

Head Case (Featuring Kendra Moreno)

Horror Emporium (Featuring K.A. Knight and Kendra Moreno)

Beloved

BELOVED

PRE-ORDER NOW (BOOKS2READ.COM/BLVD)

The world bleeds as Noble vampire families war amongst themselves. The Valentine and Bordeaux clans have fought for centuries over the right to rule. Until an opportunity to merge the two sides is born.

Sabine Bordeaux is destined to marry the Valentine heir, something she's known since birth. Their union will end the bloodshed once and for all. She knows her duty...

...and wants nothing to do with it.

She never expected three men, shrouded in mystery, to answer her prayers. Whisked away to an island she's only heard about in fairy tales, at the mercy of the very Gods she prayed to for a reprieve, secrest come to light that leave Sabine lost and confused.

She wanted to escape her duty...

She just never knew how much she'd bleed for it.

Made in the USA
Middletown, DE
14 February 2020